STORMS OF OLYMPUS

TRIALS 7, 8 & 9: HERMES, APHRODITE & ARES

ELIZA RAINE

Editors: Anna Bowles, Kyra Wilson

Cover: The Write Wrapping

HERMES

THE IMMORTALITY TRIALS

TRIAL SEVEN

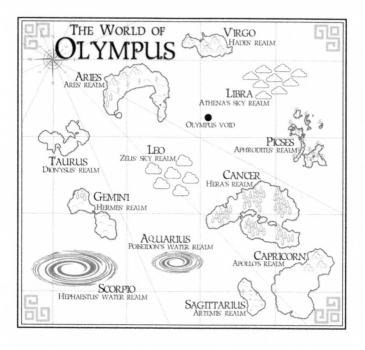

THE WORLD OF
OLYMPUS

VIRGO
HADES' REALM

ARIES
ARES' REALM

LIBRA
ATHENA'S SKY REALM

OLYMPUS VOID

LEO
ZEUS' SKY REALM

PICSES
APHRODITES' REALM

TAURUS
DIONYSUS' REALM

CANCER
HERA'S REALM

GEMINI
HERMES' REALM

AQUARIUS
POISEIDON'S WATER REALM

CAPRICORN
APOLLO'S REALM

SCORPIO
HEPHAESTUS' WATER REALM

SAGITTARIUS
ARTEMIS' REALM

1

LYSSA

Lyssa gasped as she sat upright and pain engulfed her. A wave of dizziness hit her hard and she realised too late that she was going to be sick. She turned her head, unable to register where she was, and squeezed her eyes shut as she vomited.

'Lyssa!'

She kept her eyes closed, still heaving. The pain in her chest and shoulder threatened to overcome her.

'Len! Len, she's awake!'

Lyssa felt a cool hand on her back, her body flinching involuntarily at the touch. 'Lyssa, it's Phyleus. You're all right. Lie back down, carefully.' He eased her gently onto her back, and she slowly opened her eyes to see him staring intensely back at her.

'Where am I?' she croaked.

'The infirmary, on the *Alastor*.' Her hazy memories sharpened suddenly and it was only Phyleus's firm hands that stopped her sitting up again.

'Epizon,' she gasped.

'He's going to be OK. Maybe not for a little while, but Len was able to save him.'

Relief washed through Lyssa, and for a brief moment she didn't feel her own pain. *Epizon is alive. Epizon is alive.* The words repeated themselves in her mind until she breathed too deeply and agony tore through her side.

'What's happened to me?' she whispered.

'A broken shoulder, and two broken ribs. We had to...' Phyleus looked away from her uncomfortably. 'We had to re-set your shoulder in order for it to heal properly. Len insisted you were kept unconscious, obviously.'

Lyssa looked up at him. 'We? You mean... You.'

'And Nestor. It's not an easy job.' Phyleus's face was pale. Lyssa closed her eyes.

'If Len said it needed to be done, then it needed to be done.' She paused before asking the question now ricocheting around her aching brain. 'Who won?'

'That doesn't matter now. What matters is that you get your strength back...'

Lyssa cut him off with a groan. There could only be one reason he wouldn't answer the question.

'It was him, wasn't it.' She opened her eyes, her heart sinking further at seeing Phyleus's resigned expression. He nodded.

'Stop crowding her.' Len's voice filled the small infirmary. 'She needs pain relief.' Gods, did Lyssa need pain relief.

'Have they announced the next Trial yet?' she asked.

'No, not yet,' Len replied. 'You've only been unconscious for about three hours.'

Lyssa turned her head gingerly to one side, scanning the little infirmary, hoping to see Epizon. But there was only the line of low cupboards against the wall to her right, and Phyleus and Len to her left.

'Where's Epizon?' she asked.

'He's still in the cargo deck. I didn't want to risk moving him. We've made him comfortable, though,' Len answered, leaning over her with a little dish of dark paste. The bed in the infirmary was low, so that Len could access it easily, and she realised dimly that Phyleus must be on his knees. 'Captain, I don't know when the next Trial will be but if you want to take part we may have to risk using ambrosia.'

'I thought you said once that ambrosia might kill me.' She frowned at the satyr's serious face.

'Yes, if I get the dose wrong. Which I might. That or you could develop a crippling addiction to it. But if I get it right it will heal your shoulder in a matter of hours.' He paused, then said, 'It's up to you.'

'Can we give it to Epizon?' Phyleus asked. Len shook his head. Lyssa already knew the answer.

'No,' she muttered. 'Anyone without a decent amount of ichor in their veins would be killed by ambrosia instantly. Let's not use it if we don't have to. It was hell to get hold of what little we do have, and we might have days before the next Trial. Just use whatever else you can to make this hurt less.'

OVER THE NEXT few hours she slept fitfully as Len regularly slathered the bitter-smelling salve onto the bruised skin of her shoulder and ribs. His flirty banter was gone and his care for her modesty was a relief. She'd always known he was a great medic but she had never needed his care for anything so serious before.

Whenever Len came in she asked for news of Epizon, and each time she was told he was still unconscious.

'What are his wounds?' she asked eventually, as Len stirred up more paste. He looked sideways at her.

'Aside from the lacerations on his arms and legs... his right lung was punctured. It didn't collapse, though, which meant I was able to repair it. He lost a lot of blood.'

Lyssa's stomach churned at the memory of Epizon's blood leaking into the water around him.

'But he's going to be all right?'

The satyr nodded.

'The whole crew offered to give blood for him.'

Lyssa's breath caught, pride and bone-deep emotion filling her.

'I didn't want to risk using yours or Nestor's,' continued Len, 'as I don't think ichor or centaur blood would be compatible with his. But Abderos and Phyleus saved his life with what they gave.' As a solitary tear leaked from her eye, sliding down her cheek and onto the white pillow, Len raised his eyebrows and smiled softly. 'You're surprised, Captain?'

She shook her head gently.

'No,' she whispered. 'But...' She trailed off, not knowing what to say. 'Thank you,' she finished.

'Of course,' he said, and scooped more salve into his small, furry hand.

'And if you tell anyone that you saw me cry I'll throw you overboard,' she mumbled, and the satyr laughed.

2

HERCULES

'Maybe we just smash it?' Evadne suggested, cocking her head at the white egg on the deck in front of them. Hercules scowled at her.

'Just smash a gift from the gods?' He shook his head. 'I don't think so.'

As much as he disliked it, he had to concede that the girl had been helpful on Scorpio. She claimed that the birds had become immobile when she had shot one of the telkhines that were controlling them. Although he had no specific reason to disbelieve her, she had been alone, and he struggled to trust her. But given that she had retrieved the egg from the nest he had opted not to push her story.

If only she could work out what the egg was for.

'Maybe it will hatch on its own?' Asterion said. They both looked at the minotaur. He shrugged. 'Maybe not.'

'I'll go and see if there's anything in any of the books about Olympus that might help,' said Evadne. She turned to Hercules and inclined her head slightly. 'With your leave, of course, Captain.'

Hercules smiled. The girl was learning. At last. He

nodded at her and she turned, making her way to the hauler.

'You may go too, Asterion. Watch the flame dish,' he said, and dismissed the minotaur with a wave of his hand.

'Captain,' grunted Asterion, then clopped across the planks towards the quarterdeck. Hercules bent over and picked up the egg, tossing it from hand to hand. What was in it? Did they need it for the rest of the Trials? He snorted. Of course he didn't need it. It was evident that he needed no help in the Trials. Lyssa had been ahead for one Trial, only one, before he was back out in front. Well, maybe not in front yet, but he soon would be. He let out a long, satisfied breath as he pictured his daughter swimming desperately towards him, fear and anger etched into her pale face. He hoped her large friend had not survived.

The egg was big, almost as large as a human head, but it weighed hardly anything. It probably floated, he thought, as he strode to the railings and looked out over the sparkling ocean. They were the only ship still so close to the surface of the water. He saw no reason to leave yet, though. For the last few Trials they had been given plenty of time to reach their destinations. Maybe he *should* just smash the egg, he thought. He stared at it for a moment more, then made up his mind. He would wait for Evadne, to see if she came up with anything from those books of hers. He was in no hurry.

ERYX

'Captain?' Eryx called tentatively through the closed door. There was silence. He waited, silently praying that Antaeus would respond.

'You're wasting your time,' said Busiris.

Eryx whirled around, realising that the gold-skinned half-giant was behind him, leaning languidly against the corridor wall. He scowled.

'You don't know that.'

'I'm his first mate; of course I know that,' responded Busiris. 'If he won't answer me through mind talk, he's not going to answer you banging at his door.'

Eryx stamped his foot, the feeling of uselessness spilling into anger.

'What do we do, then?' he snapped. Busiris shrugged.

'We do nothing. There is nothing we can do.'

Eryx narrowed his eyes and made to stomp past him but Busiris shot out his arm, catching Eryx by the shoulder. 'I saw her, you know,' he said quietly.

Eryx's heart skipped a beat. He tried not to swallow as he stared into Busiris's glittering black eyes.

'Saw who?' he said blithely. Busiris gave a low, sarcastic chuckle.

'You're a fool, Eryx, no doubt about that, but even you can't be that stupid.'

Anger clamped around Eryx's chest, his muscles tensing.

'Don't call me—' he started, but Busiris cut him off.

'Don't call me stupid,' he parroted, his voice high pitched in mockery. 'I know, I know. You don't like to be called stupid. But by letting her play you, you are proving that you are. And you're risking the entire crew's shot at the prize. Look at what she did to our longboat.'

'I don't know what you're talking about,' Eryx hissed.

'We both know that you do, Eryx. And if you see her again, make no mistake, our captain will know too.' Eryx bit his tongue in an effort to keep his mouth shut, turning away from Busiris's cold gaze and storming up the corridor. Who did that slimy cretin think he was to threaten him? Still, unease and guilt trickled through Eryx like ice water down his spine. Busiris was right to tell Antaeus. He already should have, in fact. Eryx himself would have done, if he'd seen his crew-mates meeting with the competition in secret.

He reached the door to his room and kicked it open, snarling. He knew Evadne was using him. He had no intention of seeing her again. In fact, he had never made any effort to see her himself. But... But what if Hercules *did* hurt her? What if she came to him one day and really needed his help? He didn't think she was lying about her captain. The impression she had given him about her feelings for him may be false, but he believed her fear of Hercules was real enough.

He threw himself down, hard, onto his bed, frustration making all of his movements too fierce. He had bigger things to worry about just now, with Antaeus refusing to talk to anybody and two of the four crews ahead of them in the Trials. They needed a win, and they needed one soon. That Trial should have been theirs, he thought, glaring at the planks lining the ceiling. Antaeus knew it, that's why he was taking this so badly. Scorpio, the forges, the net... They should have won. They nearly did, until... Until Evadne disabled the telkhine and won it for the *Hybris*. He closed his eyes and swallowed, his resolve hardening. She was his enemy. She had made a fool of him right back at the beginning, before they had even left for the first Trial. He couldn't, *wouldn't* trust her. Even if she was the only woman he'd ever played dice with. The only woman who had ever spent time with him outside of his bed. The only woman who had gotten so utterly *stuck* in his head.

No, he scolded himself, halting his train of thought. Evadne was Hercules's pet and Busiris was right. He couldn't see her again.

HEDONE

Hercules had won. Hedone hugged her legs tighter to herself, letting out a small squeak of delight. He would be so happy! She wished she could be with him, to celebrate his victory, to hear his rich laugh, to see the power glittering in his eyes...

But she was alone, in her bed on the *Virtus*. Her smile faltered slightly. Soon. Soon the opportunity would arise and Hercules would be ready for her to join him on the *Hybris*. And until then she would think about him, imagine his face, his strong arms, his hands... Hedone lay back on the bed and closed her eyes, losing herself in her fantasy.

'HEDONE?' The voice in her head woke her from sleep. 'Hedone? The flame dish, you're going to miss it.'

It was Theseus. The flame dish... She leaped from her bed and, not bothering to change from her silk nightgown, ran to her door. She yanked it open and dashed to the hauler. When she burst onto the quarterdeck the blond announcer was just fading from sight, his image being replaced by red-haired Hermes. The god's twinkling green eyes flashed as he spoke.

'Good day, heroes. You have done well, so far. As god of trickery, wit and thievery, though, I have something a bit different planned for you. I have a built a labyrinth in Crete, on the south island of Gemini, for you all to solve. At the centre will be a priceless gem, guarded by my own pet bull. If you can pass the tests and traps in the maze you will receive keys. If you can find the centre of the maze and pass the bull, you will need two keys to release the gem. If you do so, you will win. And, of course, you can keep the gem.' He winked, running his hand through his short beard. 'Finders keepers, and all that. The coloured lights will show you where to start. Good luck.' Hermes faded from the flames, and Hedone watched them settle again, crackling quietly.

'This is the perfect Trial for you, Captain,' said Bellerephon, smiling.

'It sounds like it,' Theseus agreed, pushing his hands through his hair and leaning back in the captain's chair. The deck moved beneath her feet and Hedone watched the orange clouds swirl past them as the *Virtus* picked up speed. They were on their way to Gemini. She looked back at her captain's serious face.

'You don't look convinced,' she said.

'I just don't want to take anything for granted. We've only won a single Trial so far, and Hercules is level with the *Alastor* again.' Hedone suppressed the little shiver that came with hearing Hercules's name on another's lips.

'If we don't win, I hope the *Alastor* does,' said Psyche, leaning back against the railings of the narrow quarterdeck. Hedone looked at her sharply and the woman put her hands in the air, raising her eyebrows. 'No need to look at me like that, I'm sure we will be victorious,' Psyche said, mistaking her anger for a desire to win.

'Why the *Alastor*?' Hedone asked quietly.

'I like Lyssa. She's strong, and, I think, a decent person, despite her chosen line of work.' Psyche shrugged.

'I spoke with her navigator, in the cage on Capricorn,' said Theseus. 'He was sold to the gladiator pits on Aries when he was a child, and Lyssa found him and took him in. She would only have been a child herself when Hercules killed her mother and brother.'

Something pulled at Hedone's gut, hard, and for a split second she felt sick. Who could do something so vile? But almost as soon as the thought settled, it floated away, and all she could grasp at was a distant knowledge that something wasn't right. Her frustration must have shown on her face because Psyche stepped towards her, frowning.

'There are many evil, corrupt people in Olympus,' she said softly. 'Don't let their deeds bring you down.' Hedone looked at her, trying to cling to the unease, to understand it. Hercules had been forced to kill his family. Hera had made him do it, turned Olympus against him. She nodded mutely, and the tenderness in Psyche's usually strong face made her eyes sting with hot tears.

'Do you want to train?' Hedone forced the question out. She needed to distract herself. She needed to be strong. Psyche raised her eyebrows in surprise.

'Yes. Of course,' she replied, cocking her head with a small smile. 'I'll fetch the spears, you go and get dressed.'

EVADNE

E vadne had pored over all the books in Hercules's rooms but nothing had given her any ideas about what to do with the egg. They were on their way to Gemini now, moving fast, and she didn't think she was going to work it out before the next Trial. A sliver of fear rippled through her as she wondered what might happen if they found out that they needed whatever was in the egg for this Trial. Would Hercules blame her for not being able to open it? She knew he would. She closed a book of hymns to the gods and set it down on the little glass table next to her chair.

'How much further?' she asked Asterion, in her mind.

'Thirty minutes,' he answered gruffly. She stood up and stretched. Her legs ached from swimming and running. Shooting down that telkhine and enabling their win should have put her back in Hercules's favour. She had not expected lavish praise or thanks, but she had expected some attention. Some special treatment. But Hercules had not asked her to his rooms to celebrate, as he did after their first win. He had not looked at her with respect for what she had worked out, for the part she had played. In fact, he'd pretty much ignored her since they had been back on the *Hybris*. With the exception of gloating over injuring Lyssa and likely killing her first mate, he had barely spoken to Evadne.

She clenched her fists and screwed up her face in over-whelming frustration. After the stables, she had wanted to keep her distance, wanted him to ignore her. But now... The way Theseus looked at Psyche with so much respect, the way Lyssa had risked her own life for Epizon's... She shook her head, hard. The need for recognition, for her achieve-ments to be acknowledged, was irrational, she told herself crossly, and picked up the book. Immature, even. For her safety and for the prize, this was best. *Stay out of his way, and keep being useful*, she chanted in her head, sliding the book back into its place on the shelf. But resentment burned under the sensible words and she couldn't shake the jeal-ousy she felt when she thought of the other crews.

'WELL?' Hercules asked her when she stepped onto the quarterdeck.

She shook her head.

'I'm sorry, Captain, there's no reference to anything useful.'

He stared at her for a moment, his grey eyes flashing, then stood up from his captain's chair. Ati leaped off his lap with a squeak and scampered to the hauler.

'We break it, then,' he said, and to her relief strode straight past her. He set the egg down gently on the deck, then drew *Keravnos* from its sheath. It glowed a faint red as he rested the tip of the sword against the shell, then pushed. A thin, perfect line crept out from where the sword pierced it and then, abruptly, the egg fell open in two pieces. Putting aside her surprise at how careful Hercules had been, Evadne leaned down to look.

There was a bottle, full of bright turquoise liquid that shimmered in the passing light.

'What is it?' asked Asterion. Evadne shrugged.

'No idea. Captain?'

Hercules was silent for a moment before he spoke.

'I'm sure it will be very valuable to me, whatever it is. Asterion, secure it in the hold.'

'Yes, Captain,' said the minotaur. He picked up the bottle gingerly, then carried it to the hauler.

EVADNE WATCHED HIM GO, breathing calmly despite her racing heart. She *did* know what was in the bottle. She had recognised it immediately. It was anapneo, a tonic that allowed the drinker to breathe under water for a time. And it was worth a *fortune*. That bottle could be her ticket off the *Hybris*, should she ever need it. It would make her rich, and while wealth wasn't immortality, it was better than nothing. Evadne was just considering following Asterion down to the cargo deck so that she could see where the tonic would be stowed when Hercules called to her. She turned to him, her face an impassive mask.

'Have you been to Gemini before?' he asked her, staring out at the clouds as they raced past. Evadne nodded.

'Yes, Captain, but only the north island. I understand the south island is mostly jungle.'

'Hermes didn't say anything about number of crew members. I'm taking you with me.'

'Yes, Captain,' she answered. He looked at her and her breath caught at the intensity in his eyes.

'Evadne.' He spoke quietly. Was he going to thank her? She held her breath. 'Don't let me down,' he said.

Evadne's insides clenched and it was all she could do not to let the anger show as her lips tightened involuntarily.

'Yes, Captain,' she ground out, and turned to follow Asterion.

Many people visited the temple of Hermes and offered him gifts in return for wisdom. When they arrived on the chosen day for the god of wisdom, eloquence and rewards, to distribute this wisdom, Hermes gifted philosophy on the person who had made the richest offering. The next best was given the ability to speak well. The rest were given gifts of astronomy or made poets, writers or musicians.

EXCERPT FROM

LIFE OF APOLLONIUS OF TYANA BY PHILOSTRATUS

Written 1–2 AD

Paraphrased by Eliza Raine

6

LYSSA

'W ow. It really is a jungle,' said Phyleus, leaning
over the railings of the *Alastor* to look down at
Gemini.

'You don't say,' answered Lyssa, who was crouching
down on the deck so Len could reach her. She couldn't
really move her arm much, and her broken ribs made
walking painfully slow, but she had to compete in the Trial.
Epizon was supposed to be in charge if she couldn't be, and
he was still under Len's care in the cargo deck. Apparently
he had woken a few times and the satyr assured her he was
doing well, but when she'd crept in to see him earlier he
hadn't stirred.

'You shouldn't be going down there, Captain,' Len said,
tightening the fabric sling across her shoulder, then stepping back and eyeing the purple beam of light they were
heading towards.

She waved her good hand dismissively.

'Hermes said it would be tests and traps. That doesn't
sound physical.'

Phyleus looked at her.

'It does sound physical, Lyssa.'

'Captain!' she corrected him sharply.

'And the gem is guarded by a bull. Your ability to escape a charging bull right now is questionable,' he carried on, ignoring her correction.

'Captain?' Nestor trotted up to her. 'I believe I have a solution for your condition.'

'I'm not drinking ambrosia. Not if I can help it...' started Lyssa, but the centaur shook her head.

'You may ride on my back,' she said.

Lyssa's eyebrows shot up and Len whirled around to face her in shock. Centaurs usually barely conversed with humans. To let one ride on their back... It was unheard of.

'Why? Why would you let me do that?' breathed Lyssa.

'I believe you would do the same for me. Or any of this crew,' Nestor said simply.

Lyssa nodded slowly.

'Thank you, Nestor. I... It might make all the difference. Len, I'd like it if you came too. You know more about Olympus than I do and if there are tests—'

'No, Captain.' Len shook his head. 'I can't leave Epizon. He's not stable enough yet.'

'Good job I know loads about Olympus, then,' said Phyleus with a lazy smile.

'I thought you wanted to sit a few Trials out?' Lyssa said, turning to him. 'Doesn't a prince need plenty of beauty sleep?' She was teasing, but she realised as she spoke that she did want him to come.

'I never said that. And I clearly don't need any beauty sleep.' He flashed her a grin and pushed his hair back from his forehead. 'Besides, I didn't do the last Trial.'

'Hmmm. You got wet all the same,' said Lyssa. *While saving my life*, she thought.

'I'm coming. And you can't stop me.' His lips didn't move as his voice sounded in her head and the anger she expected to feel at being told what she could and couldn't do didn't come. His eyes flashed as she stared at him, defiance playing across his face.

'What have I told you about talking to me like this!' she shot back mentally.

'You need me.' His gaze deepened and heat flooded her cheeks. His desire was clear in his eyes. She didn't know if she needed him or not, but it was getting harder to deny that she *wanted* him.

'Fine, Phyleus, you can come,' she said aloud, breaking eye contact with him. 'Ab, how long until we get there?'

'About fifteen minutes, Captain,' Abderos said from the wheel behind her.

'All right,' she breathed.

Lyssa winced as Phyleus helped pull her into the longboat. The *Alastor* would never get low enough through the dense jungle foliage to let them reach the ground, so the longboat was their only option, even though Nestor almost filled the little craft. Lyssa willed the boat up and off the main deck of the ship, towards the purple beam erupting from the green trees below the ship.

'Good luck, Cap!' yelled Abderos as they sailed off.

She leaned over the boat's edge, watching the trees part slightly as they neared the light. A pale yellowing stone could be seen through gaps in the canopy. It was some sort of structure.

'I guess that's the labyrinth?' said Phyleus, leaning over beside her.

'Mazes are simple,' said Nestor. They both looked at her.

'Choose one wall and always turn right. It will not be the shortest route, but you will not get lost.'

'Huh,' said Phyleus. 'That kind of makes sense.'

Lyssa frowned. It wasn't the way she had planned to tackle the labyrinth, but she was willing to give it a go. Centaurs were known for their wisdom, after all.

When they reached the beam of light she lowered the boat, carefully manoeuvring through the trees. It got hotter as they descended and within moments her shirt was damp and sticking to her skin. She was glad she had worn cotton trousers; leather would have been awful in the humidity. Birds called loudly to each other and once they were fully through the thick canopy the light got darker and a strong smell of earth invaded her nostrils. Lyssa landed the small boat in a clearing right at the base of the beam of light, which was shooting up directly from a forest floor littered with leaves and roots and things that scuttled.

'There.' Phyleus pointed to two tall trees with a narrow gap between them, a yellow stone wall just visible beyond. 'The labyrinth.'

7

LYSSA

L yssa couldn't help feeling awkward as she tried to settle herself on Nestor's broad back. The centaur had barely said a word when Phyleus had given her a leg up and she'd gripped the centaur's flank with her good arm and heaved herself into a sitting position. Now she held onto Nestor's sturdy belt, careful not to touch her human back.

'You look uncomfortable,' Phyleus said to her mentally as they approached the entrance to the maze.

'You think?' Lyssa snapped. He threw her a smile and they stepped between the trees.

'LEFT OR RIGHT?' Phyleus said as he looked both ways down the endless pale stone corridor. Lyssa glanced up in relief at the swirling pastel sky visible through overhanging trees, saying a silent thanks that they weren't underground or closed in.

'Right,' said Nestor.

'OK,' Phyleus replied, turning to his right and walking forward confidently.

'Hermes said there would be traps. Go carefully,' Lyssa warned. Phyleus looked back and rolled his eyes at her.

'Yes, Captain,' he drawled and took a few exaggeratedly slow steps forward. Nestor overtook him in a couple of strides and he made a noise of protest. Lyssa suppressed a small laugh. They walked in silence for a while, then Phyleus stopped suddenly, pointing.

'Look.'

There was an archway in the wall to their left, and Lyssa peered at it as Nestor slowed to a stop. The columns of the arch were carved with snakes and midway up were two huge stone lion heads.

'Do we go through?' Lyssa asked.

The second she stopped speaking the lion heads shimmered, like a wave of heat had hit them, then they grew, coming away from the columns. Nestor stepped back quickly as two full-size lions slowly emerged from the stone, stretching and pawing at the ground. Wings sprouted slowly from their backs, and as she watched their faces morphed and changed until they looked human.

'Sphinxes,' whispered Nestor. One of them looked at her sharply, then sat back on its haunches, tucking in its wings. The second took up the same position on the other side of the archway.

'They still look like they're made from stone,' breathed Phyleus in awe.

'We are made from stone,' the creatures said in unison, their voices weirdly lyrical, followed by an unnatural echo. Phyleus jumped and Nestor took another step back, bumping her hind legs against the opposite wall of the corridor.

'Where does this archway lead?' Lyssa asked them.

'Where you need to go,' they answered, without looking at her.

'May we go through?'

'If you pass the test.'

'OK. What's the test?' Lyssa asked the sphinxes. Their eyes started to glow red and when they spoke their voices were louder.

'WHEN THE HEROES are put to the test
    Their knowledge of gemstones must be the best
    From each of the stones, take the first letter
    You're left with a word that's in every way better
    The first is divine, with colours of rainbow
    The second is white with a bright blue glow
    The third is green, wrapped in stripes and lines
    The fourth is dark but the black still shines
    The fifth is rich in red, like blood
    The sixth is the blue of an ocean flood
    The seventh is purple, clear and bold
    The eighth is dark blue, shot through with gold
    The last is true blue: most precious of all
    What word will allow you to pass through the wall?'

PHYLEUS LOOKED UP AT LYSSA.

'Gemstones?' she groaned. She knew nothing about gemstones.

'At least it's not physical.' He shrugged.

'Gods, why don't we have Len? He would have known all of these,' she sighed. She'd tried to make mental contact with her crew already but, like in many of the Trials so far, there was no response.

'You underestimate your company, Captain. Wealthy prince, remember.' Phyleus grinned at her.

'I think I know some of these,' Nestor said. 'If the first is divine and rainbow coloured, it must the rainbow goddess' gem, Iris stone.'

'The fourth is black and shiny, so Onyx.' Phyleus nodded. 'The blood-red one has got to be a Ruby.'

'Seventh is purple and clear, so Amethyst?' added Nestor.

'Definitely,' said Phyleus, rubbing his chin as he thought. 'True blue and most precious, that'll be Sapphire. What was the order again?' He turned to the sphinxes.

'We will not tell you more than three times,' they said, then repeated the puzzle.

'OK, dark blue and gold is probably Lapis Lazuli,' Phyleus said, frowning in concentration.

'What in Olympus is Lapis Lazuli?' asked Lyssa.

'Don't distract me,' Phyleus muttered. Lyssa scowled at him, but held her tongue.

'Blue like an ocean flood might be Turquoise. Or Topaz,' said Nestor.

'Well, it doesn't matter which, we need the first letter and they're the same,' Lyssa said.

'Excellent.' Phyleus beamed. 'I think green with stripes must be Malachite.'

'Is that all of them?'

'No.' Nestor shook her head. 'White with a bright blue glow.' They all fell silent.

'Well, what letters do we already have? Maybe we can work it out from those,' Lyssa offered eventually.

'We have Iris stone, Ruby, Amethyst, Onyx, Sapphire, Turquoise, Malachite...' Phyleus trailed off.

'Lapis Lazuli,' said Lyssa.

'Oh yeah. We need the order again.'

'It's the last time,' warned Nestor.

'We'll just have to hope we get it right, then. Can we have the riddle again?' Lyssa asked. The creatures' eyes glowed again as they repeated the riddle. Phyleus followed along, ticking off the gems.

'I, something, M, O, R, T, A, L,' he said slowly.

'Immortal,' breathed Lyssa. 'A word which is in every way better. The word is "immortal".' As she said it, the sphinxes began to shrink, folding backwards and disappearing into the stone pillars.

'What was the missing gem?' called Phyleus.

'What does it matter?' Lyssa said incredulously. 'We solved it!'

'Moonstone.' The voice of the sphinxes carried quietly over as they melted into the arch completely, becoming just large lion heads carved into the stone once again.

'Of course! Moonstone,' Phyleus said, putting his hand to his head. 'I'm sure I would have worked it out eventually.' Lyssa shook her head at him.

'Look.' Nestor pointed at the lion head on the left. One of its eyes was different, made from something other than the yellow stone of its body. It glittered in the filtered light, but Lyssa was positioned too high up to see it clearly. Phyleus stepped up to the head and laughed aloud as he peered at it.

'It's the key,' he said, prising a dark blue orb out of the stone lion's eye socket, then tossing it up to her. 'And it's made from Lapis Lazuli.' Lyssa caught the orb with her good hand, and held it up to the light. It was beautiful. Most of it was a solid, deep rich blue, but veins of sparkling gold weaved across the smooth surface. Mesmerised, she turned it around in her hand, watching the gold streaks sparkle like the dust that they flew past in the sky.

'It's stunning,' she breathed.

'Yes. We need to go, Captain,' said Nestor, almost causing Lyssa to drop the ball as she strode towards the archway. Lyssa huffed but said nothing as she placed the key carefully in the pouch on her belt and they passed through the arch.

8

HEDONE

'Captain, we should have come across something by now,' said Psyche warily.

Hedone thought she was right. There had been nothing but bare stone walls for corridor after corridor so far. She looked up at the leafy branches overhead. They were starting to thin out the further into the maze and away from the rest of the jungle they got.

'Maybe the maze itself is enough of a test?' she suggested.

'No.' Theseus shook his head, a few steps in front of her. 'We need to collect two keys.' There was a loud cranking noise behind them and they all spun around to look. A wall was rising from the dusty floor, sealing the corridor behind them.

'What—' Hedone turned back as a new noise started, to see an identical wall rising slowly in front of them. 'What's happening?'

'Here, look,' Bellerephon said. Hedone turned to see a chunk of the corridor on her left dropping into the floor, as fast as the other two walls were rising.

'It's a door. It seems we're supposed to go this way,' muttered Theseus, pushing his braids back from his face and stepping towards the growing doorway. Hedone shifted her spear into her other hand and frowned at the new walls in front of and behind them.

'We don't have much choice,' she said.

THESEUS STEPPED through the dark doorway first, and light immediately flooded the room. Bellerephon followed him, and then Psyche and Hedone stepped through together, and the cranking started up again. The doorway was rising, blocking the exit. Hedone resisted the instinctive urge to jump the lip of stone, to get back to the corridor and avoid being trapped. If she did that, she'd probably just get stuck out there instead.

She looked around the new room. They were standing on more dusty stone but in front of them, a few feet away, was a pool of gently lapping water. A rickety-looking rope bridge ran over the pool to the other side of the room, where a huge statue of a phoenix was carved from the stones of the wall itself. Its wings were spread out enough to reach the edges of the room and its beak was wide open.

'Look at its eyes,' muttered Psyche. Hedone squinted at the statue's face, then jumped as red flashed in the bird's eyes and a voice boomed from nowhere.

'Pay the price for your success.'

'Was that the statue talking?' asked Hedone, eyebrows raised.

'It doesn't matter. We need to work out what to do,' answered Theseus, turning away from the phoenix. 'Look.'

Hedone followed his pointing finger. Behind them, either side of where the doorway had been, were two tall cylindrical stone basins, catching coloured liquid that flowed from small openings in the wall. The liquid on the left was a glittering silver, and the liquid on the right was a rich gold. A jug was stood against the base of each basin. Theseus stepped up to the basin containing the silver liquid and bent over to pick up the jug. He scooped some of the water into it and then poured it back into the bowl. Then he walked over to the gold liquid and did the same.

'Maybe we need to mix them,' he said quietly.

'What for?' Psyche asked, raising her eyebrows sceptically. He shrugged.

'Pay the price for your success.' He repeated the words they had heard. 'This stuff is gold and silver.'

'You're suggesting that the liquid is money?'

'Maybe.'

Hedone turned back to the phoenix statue across the pool.

'Do we pay the statue?' she asked.

'There's nothing else in here, so I guess so,' Theseus answered.

'Maybe we pour the liquid into its beak?' she suggested.

'Worth a try.' Psyche shrugged and reached out for the jug. Theseus filled the one he was holding with gold liquid and passed it to her.

'Take this,' she said to Hedone and thrust her spear out. Hedone took it with her empty hand and Psyche stepped up to the bridge and wiggled the metal poles holding the rope handrail up. The metal didn't move and she nodded. She put one gold-booted foot on the first plank hesitantly and the wood creaked loudly. Gripping the rope, she took a slow step forward. The was a loud crack and Hedone gasped as Psyche's boot went through the plank and into the water below with a splash. Smoke began issuing from the water and Psyche yelled, hanging onto the rope handrail and flailing the jug in the other. Dropping the spears on the ground with a thud, Hedone darted forward, almost colliding with Bellerephon. He reached Psyche first, taking the jug from her and hauling her back onto the stone bank. The gold armour around Psyche's foot and up her shin was smeared in black, no longer gleaming.

'I think it's acid,' Psyche breathed as they all stared at it.

'If you hadn't had your armour on...' Hedone started the sentence but didn't finish it.

'It's my armour that caused the bridge to break. It's too heavy.'

Everybody looked at her and Hedone gulped.

'And I'm the lightest,' she said slowly.

'Just see if the bridge takes your weight. We'll be right there if you need us,' said Theseus gently. Hedone took a deep breath. This was good, she told herself. She could take ages, and then Hercules would have a better chance of winning. Finding ways to slow her own crew down was the only reason she was getting so involved with the Trials.

'OK,' she said. 'Give me the jug.' Bellerephon held it out to her and she took it, wincing at the weight. She would normally carry something this heavy with two hands.

SHE STOOD at the start of the bridge, holding the rope with one hand, and stretched her leg out over the now-missing first plank. She brought her foot down as lightly as she could on the next one, pushing tentatively. It creaked a little, but not as much as when Psyche had tried.

'We're right here, I've got you,' Psyche said from directly behind her, and planted both hands reassuringly on her hips, ready to pull her back. With a final long breath out,

Hedone pushed her foot down onto the plank and let the wood take her weight. She felt Psyche's grip on her tighten for a moment, but the wood held.

'I think it's OK,' she said, and tried to grip the other rope handrail while holding the jug. Gold liquid splashed out of it and hissed as it hit the water below. Hedone ignored it and lifted her other leg off the stone edge and onto the next plank. She felt Psyche's hands leave her and heard the woman make an anxious noise. But the wood only protested slightly, and Hedone reached for the state of concentration she had achieved when scaling the mountain on Capricorn. *One leg in front of the other*, she chanted in her head, as she shuffled her hands down the coarse rope, ignoring the liquid slopping from the jug. There was no way she could do this without holding the rail on both sides. She would just have to lose some liquid on the way and make more trips.

AFTER COUNTING TEN PLANKS, Hedone was relieved when her foot connected with hard stone. She held onto the metal poles at the end and pulled herself off the bridge, onto the narrow bank in front of the statue. She had to stand on tiptoes, and the jug was only half full, but as she poured the gold liquid into the phoenix's beak there was a familiar whirring sound.

'The door's opening!' called Psyche.

'It's working,' breathed Theseus. 'The eyes are starting to glow.'

Checking the jug was empty, Hedone stepped back a little to look at the statue's eyes. He was right. A deep red glittered back at her.

9

ERYX

E ryx leaped backwards as Antaeus roared with
frustration and launched a heavy metal cog across
the small room. It clanged loudly against the
yellowing stone, then hit the floor and rolled soundlessly
back towards them.

Eryx bent over and picked it up, then stared ahead with
a sigh. The room was empty except for one wall, which was
covered in short pins all holding up different-sized cogs. In
the top right-hand corner of the room there was a small cage
on a pulley, far too high for any for them to reach. In the
bottom left-hand corner there was a rotating handle,
attached to a fixed cog. Busiris had worked out quickly that
they needed to arrange all of the cogs so that the bottom
handle would turn them all in sequence, right up to the top
pulley, which would lower the cage. But they had yet to
succeed.

'I thought you said this would be easy,' Antaeus growled
to Busiris.

'Too many of the cogs are similar-sized,' he replied
gruffly. 'We'll just have to keep trying.' Busiris snatched the

cog from Eryx and walked up to the wall, pulling another
cog – apparently identical – off a pin and replacing it with
the one Antaeus had thrown.

'We're going to be here forever,' Eryx groaned.

'Shut up and try the handle,' Busiris answered, stepping
back and squinting at the wall. Eryx sighed again but did as
he was told. Nothing happened.

'If that one was there and this one was here...' Busiris
mumbled to himself and pulled more cogs off pins. 'Captain, put this one here, please,' he said, handing a large cog
to Antaeus and pointing above his own head to a pin he
couldn't reach. Antaeus snatched the cog from him and
scowled as he pulled off the current one.

'This is a ridiculous test,' he barked. Busiris glanced up
at him as he rearranged more cogs.

'It's a different kind of test. So far, a lot less lethal than
previous ones,' he said. 'Eryx, try again.'

Eryx pushed the handle half-heartedly, and started
when he felt some resistance. He pushed harder and Busiris
clapped his hands together.

'That's it!' he exclaimed. The cogs were turning! The
cage was slowly lowering on its rope and Eryx wound the
handle faster, until Antaeus could reach it. His captain tore
open the little grate on the front of the cage and pulled out a
tiny glowing sphere.

'A key,' said Eryx. It was much, much smaller than the
one he had got from the Hydra or the ones for the ice cage
on Capricorn. Antaeus held it out to Busiris.

'Look after it. It's too small for my pockets,' he said, and
dropped the ball into Busiris's hands. Eryx felt a twinge of
jealousy but pushed it down. In fairness to Busiris, he had
solved the test.

.   .   .

THERE WAS A WHIR, and Eryx turned to see the doorway that had sealed itself when they entered the cog-filled chamber reappearing behind them. It was hard not to feel a wave of relief at being able to leave the little room. There were not many trees overhead any more and the sky above was turning a deeper shade of orange, darkening the labyrinth and making it feel smaller. Eryx could understand his captain's frayed temper. This was no place for a large man, let alone a full-sized giant.

'I'm glad this maze has no roof,' he said, out loud. 'It would feel even smaller than it already does. Nice to see some sky.' He forced some optimism into his voice.

Antaeus grunted but said nothing, staring at the growing doorway.

10

EVADNE

E vadne stood back, arms folded tightly across her leather vest. Hercules was not a stupid man, of that there was no doubt. But his strength clearly didn't lie in playing children's games. He had been standing in front of the huge stone puzzle for at least twenty minutes and she had no intention of offering him any help until he asked her for it. She knew it was a foolish thing to do, but she couldn't help it. The longer she watched him pulling out the hand-sized tiles, brightly painted with intertwining serpents, then putting them back next to other tiles that didn't match up, the more her resolve hardened.

SHE HAD PLAYED games like this throughout her lonely childhood, and had rushed to the central table when they entered the small stone room. But Hercules had pushed her out of the way and began pulling out the tiles, moving them around before she could stop him. Now the tiles were hopelessly jumbled up and he was no closer to solving the puzzle than when he started.

'You think you could do better?' His voice startled her as he growled without turning away from the table. Her simmering resentment must have been obvious. She thought about how to answer him. Her priority should be solving the puzzle and winning the Trial. And she couldn't win a fight with him.

'I played with puzzles like this a lot as a child,' she said. Hercules stilled, then took a long step to the side of the table. He gestured at the puzzle with an outstretched arm, still not looking at her. His silence made her nervous and she felt a trickle of regret for her defiant behaviour.

'I'm sure you'll get there soon,' she said, 'but it might be quicker with two.' And she stepped up to the table.

THERE WERE five different-coloured snakes among the jumbled tiles, and she started by collecting the matching colours together in heaps. Then she sorted through the stacks, finding pieces that had blank edges and were therefore likely to sit around the edge of the picture. She moved quickly, testing tiles against each other and discarding them fast when she spotted inconsistencies. Before long she had half of the picture in place, the snakes lined up perfectly across the table. She risked a sideways glance at her captain, but his eyes were fixed on the puzzle, his jaw set and his mouth a hard line. Apprehension pulled at her gut and she refocused on placing the tiles.

'THERE,' Evadne said, slotting in the last tile and stepping back to see the full image. She heard a click and the middle four tiles in the puzzle began rising up from the table. Underneath them, a metal sphere sat in a small steel cage.

'The key!' Evadne reached forward to open the cage, but stopped herself. 'Captain,' she said, and moved away from the table. Hercules leaned over the puzzle and opened the little door on the cage, pulling out the orb and dropping it into the pouch on his belt without inspection. There was a whir and Evadne turned to see the doorway that had disappeared when they entered the room slowly begin reforming in the wall.

'Evadne,' Hercules said quietly and she faced him.

The look in his eyes turned her blood cold.

'I believe you are trying to make a fool of me.'

She shook her head emphatically, her stomach lurching involuntarily.

'No, Captain, of course not.'

'You could have offered your knowledge of these games much earlier than you did. Why did you not tell me earlier you knew how to solve it?' He still spoke quietly, and it scared Evadne so much more than if he were shouting.

'I... I thought you were doing well,' she stammered. Hercules didn't react, and she couldn't hold his gaze. She dropped her eyes to floor. 'I'm sorry I didn't speak sooner, Captain. I will in future.'

'Your future will be determined by me, Evadne. And at the moment, it's looking bleak.'

He strode past her to the door and she squeezed her eyes shut. She was a damn fool! What was she thinking, being so obvious, so defiant? She needed to prove that he needed her, but on his terms. She knew that. She could not allow her emotions to get the better of her again.

11

LYSSA

'Why don't we have Len with us? We would have won this bloody Trial by now,' Lyssa moaned.

They had roamed around the maze for another fifteen minutes, Nestor leading the way, and just when Lyssa was starting to feel frustratingly lost, a new doorway had appeared in the wall beside them. Walls had risen from the ground in front and behind them and they had no choice but to go through the new door, into a large room with a sandy floor. There were no trees overhead any more, and light from the orange sky shone down onto the bones that covered the sand. On the far wall of the room there was a detailed drawing of a dragon, wings raised high above its spindly neck and head. Lines had been drawn in red, pointing to various parts of the creature, and scribbled notes described the functions of its anatomy.

'I don't know how familiar Len is with dragon anatomy,' said Phyleus, peering at the drawing.

'More familiar than us, I'll bet,' she grumbled. Being stuck up on Nestor's back was making her bad-tempered. She felt useless and her arm ached like hell.

'The only thing in here is the bones. Do you think they're from a dragon?' asked Phyleus, dropping to his knees and picking up a bone longer than his arm.

'Perhaps we need to arrange them correctly,' said Nestor.

'Correctly? Like, in the shape of a dragon?' Phyleus looked at the centaur.

'Yes.'

Lyssa looked from the picture to the bones and back again. It made sense.

'Phyleus, help me down,' she said. He frowned and opened his mouth and she narrowed her eyes and bared her teeth at him. He closed his mouth again and put the bone down. 'It'll take forever going back and forth from the picture; this thing will be huge. I'll stand by the drawing and direct you two.'

'Fine.' Phyleus shrugged as he reached her. She put her good hand in his outstretched one and winced as she shifted her weight, swinging her leg over the centaur's back and facing him. Her backside was numb.

'Don't jump down or your feet will hurt like hell when they hit the ground,' Phyleus said.

'Huh. Experience riding horses?' Lyssa asked. Nestor flicked her tail and Lyssa immediately felt guilty for comparing her to a horse. 'Sorry, Nestor,' she said. The centaur didn't reply.

'Just roll off, I'll catch you,' Phyleus said. Lyssa frowned at him, not wanting to feel any more of an invalid than she already did, but the truth was that she didn't want to jump off. If her legs were as numb as her rear she would likely fall flat on her face.

'Fine,' she muttered. Phyleus stepped up close to Nestor's side and gripped her waist with his other hand as she rolled herself slowly towards him. She couldn't use her injured arm at all and her breath hitched as she left Nestor's back, but Phyleus's strong arms caught her quickly. Their faces were close and as her eyes connected with his, desire flashed inside her, so strong that it triggered her power. Strength pulsed through her muscles suddenly, delicious relief from the aches and pain. Phyleus drew a sharp breath in and she wondered if he felt it too. His eyes darkened, his lips parted and power surged from her core through her whole body.

Nestor coughed and Phyleus almost dropped Lyssa. Heat flushed her face and she struggled to pull herself out of his grip. Her feet throbbed as she stood, and she busied herself stretching her legs, avoiding looking at him.

'The spindly bones are probably the arch of the wings,' said Nestor, bending over.

'Yes,' said Phyleus, too quickly. 'Let's gather similar-looking bones together. The creature will probably be quite symmetrical; when one side is done we just need to repeat it on the other.'

Lyssa walked over to the drawing as they began gathering bones, flexing her fists and trying to shake out the energy that was pounding through her body.

12

HEDONE

Hedone felt exhausted as she poured the liquid into the phoenix statue's beak. She couldn't do many more trips across the bridge. Every crossing wracked her with nerves, relief rushing through her each time her feet were on solid stone again.

At least she was holding her crew up and giving Hercules a better chance, she thought, arm aching as she tipped the heavy jug up to get the last drops into the statue.

A loud click made her jump back in surprise. The beak was moving. It was opening. She stared as the stone parted, revealing a shining red orb the size of her palm.

It was the key.

She dropped the jug on the floor, hearing a shout of concern from Theseus behind her, and reached in for the orb. Holding it aloft, she turned and waved it at the others.

'The key!' The sense of achievement was so great as she turned and held it aloft, waving it at the others, that she couldn't keep the excitement from her voice, or her face. She felt a pang of guilt, remembering that just a moment ago she had been happy about their lack of progress, but as she looked at it the little ball pride over-powered any other emotion. She had done it! Alone, and with no help. She pushed the orb into the pouch on her belt and carefully stepped back onto the bridge, bracing herself for the final crossing, adrenaline humming through her.

As soon as she set foot on the other side, Psyche clapped her hard on the shoulder and pulled her into an embrace. Hedone was so surprised she gave a small squeak as she bumped against the woman's solid armour.

'Well done,' Psyche said, and pride welled in her again. Theseus grinned at her over Psyche's shoulder.

'You did great, Hedone,' he said as Psyche stepped back. Hedone nodded at him, then noticed the wide open doorway.

'I guess we can leave now?' she said. Theseus looked at the doorway too.

'I guess so.'

THERE WERE no trees overhead any more so she guessed they were now further from the perimeter of the maze. Theseus was in the lead, choosing the directions they took, which corridors they went down and which ones remained unexplored.

It was boring, walking through the endless passages, dull stone on either side of them. Adrenaline still pulsed through Hedone, her hands shaking ever so slightly. She needed to do something. Something other than walking aimlessly around. She thought of Hercules, wondering where he was in the labyrinth right now. Perhaps he was near her. Perhaps just the other side of one of the stone walls. She reached up as they walked, running her fingers

over the rough surface. Then the familiar whir started and
she snatched her hand back.

'Another door.' Psyche pointed. It was appearing in the
opposite wall to the one she had touched, Hedone saw,
knowing it was irrational to think she had triggered it.

'Another chance at getting a key,' said Theseus, stepping
through the growing doorway.

PRAYING it would be something Theseus couldn't solve
quickly, Hedone stepped into the room after him. A circular
pool filled most of the floor, the water moving gently. There
was space to walk around the edge of the water and she
leaned over carefully, looking in. Flashes of bright colours
zipped about, too fast to make out clearly.

'Are they fish?' she asked.

'I don't know,' muttered Theseus.

'Here,' said Bellerephon, and they both turned to him.
He was holding two nets, attached to the end of long poles.
'These were against the wall here.'

'So we have to catch them?'

Bellerephon shrugged and passed a net to Theseus. He
crouched over the pool, net poised, and watched for a
moment, completely still. Then, lightning quick, he darted
his net into the water. He pulled it out again just as fast and
Hedone's eyes widened in surprise. A bright red fish was
thrashing around in the net.

'It's pretty,' she started to say, when there was bang and
the net exploded. She screamed and threw herself against
the wall at the same time as Theseus yelled and launched
the net away from him, towards the pool.

'What happened?' she gasped.

'I don't know, it just...'

'Exploded,' finished Psyche. 'Don't catch the red ones?' she offered.

'Which ones should we catch?'

The woman shrugged and scanned the room.

'There are only four more nets. So we don't have many chances to find out.'

13

HERCULES

They had lost too much time on the first test, thought Hercules as he stamped down another stone corridor. Evadne would pay. He wasn't sure how yet, but he would think of something suitable.

He ground his teeth, his fists clenched. This cursed labyrinth wasn't helping. He was following his instincts, choosing the paths they took, but he knew enough about Hermes to be sure that it wouldn't be simple. The god of trickery would make this hard for all of them. As if on cue, a solid stone wall began rising from the ground in front of him and he stopped abruptly. It was obviously time for another test.

HERCULES DUCKED through the doorway before it had fully opened, taking in a very long, narrow room. Metal rods ran across the top of the walls, from one side to the other, and hanging from them at staggered intervals were canvas sacks on ropes. The closest was probably ten feet away, the furthest maybe a hundred. Under each sack, on the sandy floor, was a shining metal dish. He took another step into the room and held his arms out to the sides. He could almost touch both walls, it was that narrow.

'There's a bow, Captain.' He turned around at Evadne's voice. She was crouched against the wall with the slowly closing doorway, picking up a bow and a tube of arrows that was propped against the stone. 'I assume you have to hit the sacks,' she said, straightening up and handing him the weapon.

HERCULES SAID nothing as he took it from her. He notched the first arrow, aimed at the closest sack, and fired. The metal arrowhead tore through the canvas and sparkling silver sand streamed from the tear into the dish below. Nodding, satisfied, he grabbed a second arrow. The second he loosed his shot, the room tilted violently and he swore as he landed hard on his knees. He could feel heat on his face as he struggled back to his feet, the room still rocking from side to side.

'The walls are hot!' called Evadne.

Hercules looked towards the sacks. He had missed. A long snarl escaped him and he snatched a new arrow from the quiver by his feet. Widening his stance, he tried to ignore the jerking floor and aimed at the bag for the second time. On a long breath out, he fired. The room stilled as soon as the arrow thudded into the sack, and the silver sand began flowing into the dish.

'It was like the room was trying to knock us into the burning walls,' Evadne panted. 'How many arrows are there?'

Hercules looked down at the quiver.

'Ten,' he said, then looked up at the sacks. He could see eight more to hit.

*

14

ERYX

Eryx would have expected having a giant the size of Antaeus in the Trials to be a huge advantage, but that wasn't how it was working out. So far his size had either been more of a hindrance than a help, as in the longboat on Sagittarius or the ice on Capricorn; or it had just been completely irrelevant, like now.

They had found their second test, and Eryx had never felt so useless. It was a word puzzle.

fi oyu inw het mots rlista yuo illw veli fevrero

THE NONSENSE WAS LAID out on a stone table across the middle of the room and each of the letters was on its own little tile. He and Antaeus had looked at each other and shrugged when they'd entered the room, but Busiris had started towards the puzzle excitedly. Now he was rearranging the letters, muttering away to himself. Much as Eryx was loath to admit it, Busiris had proved himself the right man for the job in Hermes's Trial. Not that it was surprising, Eryx thought, as he folded his arms across his chest. Hermes was the god of trickery and deceit. Of course the slimy Busiris would have kinship with him.

ERYX SCREWED up his face and leaned back against the cool wall. He looked up at the sky, at the purples and reds folding through the deep orange glow.

'Have you been to Gemini before?' he asked Antaeus. His captain looked sideways at him, from where he leaned against the same wall.

'Only the north island. I visited the academy.'

'That's the famous school here?'

'Yeah. It's one of three. The other two are on Libra and Aquarius.'

Eryx turned to him. 'Did you go to school?'

Antaeus barked a laugh.

'No. But Poseidon made an effort to educate me where it was needed.'

Jealousy stung Eryx and he looked away. Gods chose their favourites, he reminded himself. There was no point getting upset about it.

'Where did Busiris learn all this stuff?' he asked.

'I'm royalty. I went to the academy,' Busiris said loudly.

Eryx thought about Busiris as a child, with his shining skin and jet black eyes.

'Is it mostly humans in the academies?'

'Yes. But don't worry, I wasn't bullied,' he said sarcastically, without turning away from the puzzle. 'There were far stranger creatures than me there.'

They fell silent for a moment, then Busiris exclaimed loudly, 'Aha! Of course!'

Antaeus stepped towards him. Eryx pushed himself off the wall to follow and looked down at the letters on the table.

IF YOU WIN the most trials you will live forever

A SECTION of the table began to lift from the stone, revealing another small cage. Busiris leaned towards it, and pulled out a second shining sphere.

'Another key! That's both of them,' said Eryx excitedly.

'Let's find that gem.' Antaeus nodded, turning to the now-whirring doorway.

15

LYSSA

'That has got to go there,' argued Phyleus, pulling the bone from Lyssa's hand.

'Are you an idiot? There's no way it goes there,' she answered, throwing her hand in the air in exasperation. 'You can see on the drawing...' She trailed off as he pointedly turned the bone the other way up and held it out next to the picture. He was right, she realised. She scowled and put her good hand on her hip.

'Just finish the damn puzzle,' she snapped. Phyleus gave her a sarcastic smile and headed over to the left wing of the dragon skeleton. Nestor was on the right-hand side, her front horse legs tucked beneath her and her human body bent over, recreating everything they had done on the left.

Lyssa watched as they placed the remaining bones in the spaces, crossing the fingers of her good hand. They'd thought the puzzle was complete twice already, but when nothing had happened and no doorway appeared, they assumed they had got it wrong, and started rearranging.

This time, though, the whirring started, and the doorway began to slowly grow in the wall.

'Yes!' said Phyleus, clenching his fist in victory.

'Behind you, Captain,' said Nestor, and Lyssa turned around quickly. The wings on the drawing of the dragon were rippling and its head seemed to be coming to life. She stepped back as it suddenly roared from the stone wall, launching a shining orb from its gaping mouth before solidifying into the wall again. Lyssa reached out to catch the ball but missed, and it hit the sandy floor with a quiet thud. Phyleus scrabbled to pick it up.

'Second key! Let's go find this gem!' he said with a grin.

IT TOOK them five full minutes to get Lyssa back up on Nestor's back. She ignored the protestations of her body, and did her best to ignore her proximity to Phyleus as she stepped into his cradled hands.

Her lack of control over her reaction to him was both alarming and sort of exciting. Nobody had made her feel that way, ever. Not that she was in the habit of flirting, but they did come across plenty of young men on their cargo jobs, and other than the man she had spent the night with in Pisces, she'd never felt any interest in any of them. Even that night, fuelled as it was by being in the realm of the goddess of love, hadn't felt so intense, hadn't triggered her power like this. And that was just from being close to him. What would it be like if they—

'Just the bull to find now, Captain,' said Nestor, as she stepped from the room back into the corridor. Lyssa shook her head slightly, banishing the thoughts of Phyleus swimming through her head.

'Yes. Just the bull to find,' she repeated, gripping Nestor's belt.

16

EVADNE

Evadne gasped as the room rocked hard to the left and she was flung towards the wall. She instinctively threw her hands out to steady herself and cried out when her fingertips brushed the burning hot stone. She stumbled into a crouch, then further down, hoping she would be steadier with her hands and knees on the ground. Hercules roared and she looked at him, also on his knees, trying to hold the bow steady as the room bucked and rolled. They still had three bags to go and only one spare arrow now. Curiously, the silver sand stayed perfectly still in the bowls, as if it was glued or magnetised.

'Is there anything I can do?' she asked tentatively.

'Unless you can make this infernal room stay still, no!' Hercules bellowed back. She winced at the fury in his voice. He was normally an excellent marksman; he would be finding this humiliating. She needed to do something.

SHE CRAWLED around on the stone floor, looking for

anything helpful, but there was nothing but sand and the dishes. Hercules had hit the sacks in order of distance so far, so the furthest of them were still intact. The room had lurched around more violently with each sack he had hit. A thought struck her.

'Try hitting the one that's furthest away,' she said.

He lowered the bow and looked at her, an angry frown on his face. 'What?'

'The room starts moving when you hit a bag, then stops when you hit the next one. Hitting the last one might stop the whole thing.'

He continued to frown at her.

'It can't hurt. You'll have to hit it anyway.' She tried to speak meekly but it came out as matter-as-fact as it was. Hercules screwed up his handsome face for a moment, then turned back to the sacks, holding the bow alongside his face as he aimed. He loosed the arrow and Evadne watched as it sailed towards the furthest sack. It hit with a thud and the room rolled to a stop.

'Thank the gods,' she muttered, but there were two sacks left. And there was still every chance that hitting the next one would start the room moving again. Hercules pulled one of the last three arrows from the quiver and aimed at one of the two remaining sacks. As he drew back the string the room tipped forward hard. Evadne tumbled over, yelling as she smashed into Hercules. He snarled as he dropped the bow, which began sliding down the tilting floor, away from him. Evadne slid past him as he reached for it, then he bellowed as the room began to tip in the other direction. Evadne scrabbled for purchase as she rolled back towards him, grasping for the bow as it passed her but missing. Hercules tried to get to his feet, but stumbled, throwing his arms out for balance.

'Don't touch the walls!' she yelled, trying to spin in the other direction as the floor got steeper. Hercules yanked his lion skin tight around himself and lurched for the bow.

Hercules's seventh labour was to capture the Cretan bull. Acusilaus claims it was the same bull that Zeus made carry Europa off, but others say that it was the bull Poseidon sent King Minos from the sea, to act as sacrifice. When Minos saw the beauty of the bull he kept it and sacrificed a different animal to Poseidon, which made him angry so he made the bull become savage.

EXCERPT FROM

THE LIBRARY BY APOLLODORUS

Written 300–100 BC

Paraphrased by Eliza Raine

17

LYSSA

'I think we should go this way,' said Phyleus, pointing as they came to a stop at a junction of four corridors.

'But we need to keep turning the same way,' answered Nestor, and Lyssa could feel the centaur's tail flicking behind her.

'I know that was the plan, but trust me, we should go this way,' he said, pointing down the middle path of the three ahead of them.

'Why?' asked Lyssa.

'I just... I have a feeling.' She raised her eyebrows at him.

'A feeling?'

'Yes. A strong feeling.' He glared up at her.

'Phyleus, Nestor's plan has been working up to now; why would we start doing something different, just because you have a feeling?'

Phyleus made a strangled noise and closed his eyes.

'I can't tell you here,' he said quietly. Lyssa scowled.

'Why not?'

He opened his eyes and stared meaningfully at her.

'The whole of Olympus is watching,' he said through gritted teeth. She raised her eyebrows. 'Please. Just trust me.'

'What are you not telling me that means you know how to navigate a labyrinth?' She stared at him, confused. 'I don't understand.'

'Lyssa, do you want to win this Trial or not?' he said, exasperated.

'Of course I do, but I'm not going to let your ego destroy the progress we've made so far, following Nestor's plan.'

He glared at her.

'This has nothing to do with my ego. Why don't you trust me?'

'Why should I trust you if you can't give me a good reason?'

Both of their voices were getting louder with each retort but she couldn't help it, he was so infuriating.

'The whole point of trust is that I don't need to give you a good reason!'

'No, the point of trust is—' she started, but Nestor cut her off.

'Shhhh. Did you hear that?' the centaur said, turning her head from side to side and raising her hand.

'No,' Lyssa and Phyleus answered in unison.

'Listen,' she whispered and they all fell silent.

LYSSA COULDN'T HEAR ANYTHING. In fact, when she thought about it, it was abnormally quiet. There were no trees overhead, so no jungle noises, and nothing else moving in the stone maze. She sighed. She needed to get to the bottom of whatever Phyleus was on about.

'There,' Nestor said suddenly.

'I can't hear anything,' said Phyleus.

He'd barely finished speaking when a distant snort cut through the silence. Phyleus whirled around and Lyssa looked about quickly. A red gleam far down the right-hand path caught her eye.

'Down there, on the right,' she said, pointing. The gleam was moving. In fact, she realised, it was getting closer, quickly. Another snort rang through the maze and a black mass surrounding two red eyes became clear.

'It's the bull,' breathed Nestor. 'Run!'

18

ERYX

E ryx peered cautiously around the next bend in the labyrinth, wondering where the grunts and snorts he could hear were coming from.

'It sounds like it's getting further away,' said Antaeus, strolling past him. Eryx trotted after his captain, adrenaline dancing through his veins, keeping him on his toes.

'If we can hear the bull, then we're getting close,' said Busiris, looking over his shoulder nervously. Eryx rolled his eyes.

THEY KEPT WALKING, Antaeus seemingly picking their path at random. Dead end after dead end greeted them and Eryx was becoming sick of the pale yellow stone that surrounded them on all sides. Every now and then they would hear the grunts of the bull in the distance and they started trying to head towards the sound. The sky was darkening above them, deep blue swirls now mingling with the burnt-orange clouds.

'Where is this blasted gem!' Antaeus suddenly shouted

beside Eryx. He jumped, his body tense and poised for action. 'Busiris, there must be a way to solve this maze,' Antaeus barked, turning to the half-giant. Busiris blinked up at him.

'If there is, Captain, I'm afraid I don't know it.'

'Gods be damned, I can't stand this place!' Antaeus punched the stone wall beside them as he shouted, and the crunching sound echoed dully around them. As he watched the stone crack and crumble, Eryx wondered briefly if Antaeus could punch their way to the middle of the maze. Then a very loud snort drew his attention from the wall.

'Is that...'

'Bull!' shouted Busiris, darting behind Antaeus. Eryx threw himself out of the way as a charging mass of black hurtled towards them, red eyes gleaming in the dimly lit corridor. Antaeus smashed his fists together and bellowed at the creature, anger and frustration all but visibly pouring from him. Eryx was sure the bull slowed down but it wasn't enough. The giant planted his feet and grabbed its pointed ivory horns as it dropped its head, lifting the creature off its feet and swinging it as he crouched. The massive animal squealed as it crashed into the wall, stone crumbling and raining down onto its body as it slumped. Antaeus roared and pulled it up, still gripping its horns, then swung it towards the opposite wall. The corridor was too narrow for the beast to go anywhere else, and Eryx actually felt a stab of pity as it collided with stone again, squealing even louder.

'Captain!' Busiris was shouting over the animal's shrieks. 'Captain, wait! Don't kill it! Hermes said it was his own pet bull, it would not do to kill it!'

Antaeus let go of the bull's horns and it scrabbled to its feet, causing a cascade of rubble from the ruined walls. With a furious snort it turned, limping fast back down the path, away from them.

Antaeus breathed heavily, watching it go, and Eryx looked at the broken walls. A faint light was coming from behind one of them and he moved towards it. Standing up on his toes he tried to look over the crumbling top part of the wall, but it was too high.

'Captain,' he said. Antaeus turned to him, anger still contorting his face. 'Captain, can you see what's over this wall?' Eryx asked him.

Antaeus took two long strides towards him and lifted his head to look. Eryx watched his captain's expression change.

'The biggest sapphire I've ever seen,' he breathed.

19

HEDONE

I t hadn't taken Theseus taken long to work out that they needed to catch the solitary silver fish that was darting around under the water's surface. It had taken him another net, though. Every time he tried for the right fish he either brought the net in empty or scooped up a different one by accident, launching it back into the water before it could explode. Psyche and Bellerephon had tried, but neither of them did any better. Theseus had offered the net to Hedone, but she had refused.

She didn't think she would be quick enough to throw the fish back in if she caught the wrong colour. And besides, she was quite happy, sitting by the pool, watching the fish, wasting time. Hopefully Hercules would get the gem soon and they would all be transported back to their ships. Maybe the next Trial would be somewhere a long way off, like Pisces or Virgo, and there would plenty of time for Hercules to visit her again. Her mind drifted off as she thought about him, about their visits, about his fierce eyes and powerful body...

'Yes! Captain, you've done it!' Hedone's head snapped up

at the sound of Psyche's jubilation. Theseus was pulling the net towards his other hand, a small silver fish thrashing frantically inside it. She forced a smile onto her face.

'Well done, Captain!' she said, through her fake beam. He grinned back at her and put his hand into the net. As soon as his fingers connected with the fish it shimmered, and turned into a shining silver orb.

'That's both keys; let's go,' said Psyche, heading quickly to the growing doorway in the wall. Hedone pushed herself to her feet slowly. Her muscles were beginning to ache. All the training she was doing was making her stronger, but it would take time to build up the sort of stamina her crew-mates had.

'Are you all right?' asked Psyche as Hedone stretched her arms high above her head and winced.

'Of course. That first test was a little draining.' She smiled.

Psyche's expression was warm.

'It would have been for anyone,' she said, before turning back to the door. That same pride she had felt before swelled within her and she wondered why the increasing approval she was getting from the older woman caused such a reaction in her. It wasn't Psyche she was trying to impress, she reminded herself as she followed them out into the corridor. It was Hercules.

20

ERYX

E ryx was sure that even the folk on the north island of Gemini must have been able to hear Antaeus's roar as he hit the wall. He had used most of the corridor for a run-up, dropping his shoulder and turning into the stone at the last minute. The ground shook as he made contact and the cracking rubble began to thunder down around him. Dust and sand flew up in huge clouds around them and for a long moment Eryx could see nothing at all. He waved his hands in front of his face, coughing and spluttering, able to hear Busiris doing the same.

As the dust finally settled, he peered through the huge gap in the broken wall. In the middle of a square courtyard stood a beautiful circular fountain, water cascading around a glass pedestal rising out of the middle. It was carved in the shape of mermaids, their bodies entwining in a kind of dance. And atop the pedestal, on a raised plinth, was a sapphire the size of a fist. Not a giant's fist perhaps, but definitely as big as a human's.

Antaeus stepped through the wall and reached the sapphire in a few strides. Light reflected off the gem, throwing rich blue shadows across the giant as he reached for it. A foot away his arm stopped abruptly, as though he'd hit something solid. He pushed harder but his hand didn't go any further.

'There's some sort of barrier,' he growled.

'The keys, Captain,' said Busiris, fishing in the pouch at his belt. Eryx stepped through the wall, making his way to the fountain. He looked at the glass mermaids on the pedestal. They were intricately detailed, smiling, their playful eyes clear on each face.

'I think the keys go here,' Busiris muttered, coming to stand beside him and pointing at the edge of the fountain. A groove ran around its circumference, starting on the outside edge, then spiralling around the bowl, under the water, all the way to the pedestal in the middle.

'Do it,' said Antaeus. Busiris carefully dropped the first orb into the start of the groove. They all watched as the ball rolled, picking up speed as it swirled around the bowl, shining under the clear water. When it hit the pedestal at the bottom there was a clicking sound and for a second it vanished. Then Eryx drew a breath as the little orb began to travel up the centre of the glass statue, its shape distorted through the carved mermaid figures. Finally, it reached the plinth at the top and vanished. Busiris dropped the second orb in and they watched it do the same, disappearing too when it reached the top.

Antaeus slowly reached his hand out for the sapphire again. This time, nothing stopped him from closing his fist around the glittering gem.

21

LYSSA

'Congratulations, Captain Antaeus.'

Lyssa blinked as she looked around. They were standing in a large courtyard with a beautiful round fountain in the middle and one of the surrounding stone walls smashed to rubble. Antaeus was standing next to the fountain, holding a sparkling blue sapphire in his open palm.

Lyssa's eyes flicked to the red-haired man who had just spoken. It was Hermes. She closed her eyes and let out a long breath. The giants had won. She gritted her teeth as she reminded herself that Antaeus's crew were the good guys. Better them than Hercules, she told herself, trying to squash her disappointment. But her own crew had been so close, she was sure.

She looked around the courtyard at the other heroes. Theseus, Psyche, Bellerephon and Hedone were to her left, and Psyche looked as annoyed as Lyssa felt. Hercules was on the other side of the courtyard, standing unnaturally straight and stiff. Fury poured from him so strongly that she could feel his power pulsing through the air. Hatred sharpened her gaze as she thought about Epizon, floating lifelessly in the water in a haze of blood. Hercules's cold grey eyes were resolutely fixed on Hermes alone. Evadne shifted uncomfortably by his side.

'YOU DEFEATED MY BULL, without seriously harming it, and you collected the keys. A worthy victor,' Hermes said, and Lyssa's attention snapped back to the god. She blinked, flexing her fists, trying to focus. Her eyes were drawn to the small white wings fluttering restlessly at Hermes's ankles, on his boots. 'For some, this Trial was not particularly dangerous, just frustrating. So let's add a little bit of drama, shall we? You shouldn't expect anything else from the god of trickery and deceit.' Lyssa frowned, looking back at the god's face. His eyes twinkled as he spoke. 'I am going to choose one crew member, completely at random, and they will be sent home. To their own home, safe and sound, but they will no longer be part of the Immortality Trials.'

Gasps filled the courtyard and Lyssa looked at Phyleus, her gut constricting. Nestor shifted underneath her. Send someone home? But her crew... Her crew lived on the *Alastor*. They didn't have homes to go to, and she needed them. She needed them all. Dread began to trickle through her, like ice in her veins. Hermes didn't know what this would do to the *Alastor*, it wasn't fair! The other captains had all found ships to take part in the Trials, they had gathered crews appropriate for the challenge, they *had* homes elsewhere. But it wasn't like that on the *Alastor*. They had been a crew before this ever began.

Phyleus reached up to her and she looked dumbly at

him. Indecision flashed across his face, then he grasped for her limp hand. She stared at his fingers as he gripped hers hard. He could be ripped away from her by Hermes. Any of them could. Her breathing was becoming shallow.

'Obviously, I shan't take any of the captains, and I would like to offer the winning crew a deal.' Hermes looked at Antaeus. 'Give me back that sapphire you just won, and your crew will be removed from the selection. They will all stay with you.'

Antaeus didn't hesitate, and respect pulsed through Lyssa despite her mounting anxiety.

'Here,' he said, and thrust the gem at the god. Hermes cocked his head at him, then reached out and plucked the sapphire from his palm.

'Though it's not really my thing, I do admire loyalty,' he said quietly. He waved the hand holding the sapphire and Antaeus cried out in surprise as a shower of sparkling gems rained down on him. Stones of every colour were falling from the sky and littering the dusty floor at his feet. Busiris crouched, quickly gathering the gems up with his hands, brushing off the sand he scooped up with them. Antaeus smiled, open-mouthed, and nodded at the god.

'Thank you, Hermes,' he said. Hermes shrugged, then walked slowly around the fountain, looking at each of the other captains in turn.

Lyssa felt sick. *Please*. She projected the thought at the god as hard as she could. *Please, please don't break up my family. They have nowhere to go*. If he took Epizon... Or Len... Epizon needed the medic's care. His life depended on it.

'Bellerephon,' Hermes said. Lyssa blinked. 'Sorry, Captain Theseus, but the selection has been made. Bellerephon will not be on your ship when you return.'

Theseus's mouth set in a thin line, but he nodded

respectfully at the god as Bellerephon spluttered beside him.

'You have one hour until the next Trial announcement.' Hermes vanished, and before tears of relief could spill from Lyssa's eyes, everything went black.

APHRODITE

THE IMMORTALITY TRIALS

TRIAL EIGHT

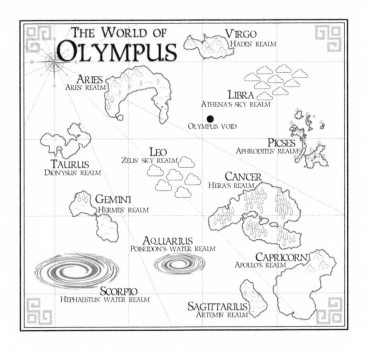

The World of Olympus

VIRGO
Hades' realm

ARIES
Aries' realm

LIBRA
Athena's sky realm

Olympus void

PICSES
Aphrodites' realm

LEO
Zeus' sky realm

TAURUS
Dionysus' realm

CANCER
Hera's realm

GEMINI
Hermes' realm

AQUARIUS
Poiseidon's water realm

CAPRICORN
Apollo's realm

SCORPIO
Hephaestus' water realm

SAGITTARIUS
Artemis' realm

1

LYSSA

Lyssa was on the deck of the *Alastor* again, still mounted on Nestor's back. The desire to feel the wood of her ship pulled at her so hard she almost fell off, Phyleus's grip on her hand the only thing steadying her.

'Whoa,' he said.

'Help me.' She couldn't keep the pleading note from her voice and he reached up quickly with his other hand, concern on his face.

'I'll always help you,' he said quietly, as she slid from the centaur's back, into his arms once more. The tears threatened again, burning at the back of her eyes, but she struggled out of his embrace, planting her boots firmly on the planks. She took a long breath, reaching out to her ship mentally, drawing its steady thrum into her mind, filling herself with its solid strength and protection. They were all here, on the *Alastor*, and they were all safe.

'You were really close, Cap,' said Abderos, as she opened her eyes and turned to see him rolling across the deck towards them. 'Like, you were definitely second.' He shrugged as he spoke. 'But Antaeus winning is all right, I s'pose.'

Lyssa closed the gap between them quickly and leaned over him, wrapping her good arm across his chest. He laughed and hugged her back, avoiding her wounded right side. 'I'm still here, Cap,' he whispered. She took a long breath, then straightened up, nodding.

'How's Epizon?' she asked.

'Erm, awake,' Abderos answered slowly.

Concern creased her face at the hesitancy in his voice.

'Is he all right?'

'He's... not quite himself. I'm sure he'll be pleased to see you, though.'

Lyssa turned to the hauler, then caught herself and turned back.

'You did great, Nestor. We couldn't have done so well without you.'

The centaur scowled back at her.

'We achieved nothing at all,' Nestor said. Lyssa winced at her words. She was right. Coming second meant nothing.

'Next time,' she said firmly and turned back to the hauler.

PHYLEUS JOGGED ACROSS THE DECK, coming to a stop in the hauler beside her. She looked at him as they began to move down, suddenly very aware that they were alone together.

'We need to finish the conversation we started,' he said. She nodded.

'Right. The one where you explain how you can navigate labyrinths.'

He shook his head.

'I can't navigate labyrinths, Lyssa.'

'Then why did you say you could?'

'I didn't. I said I knew which way to go to get to the gem.'

'Captain?' Len's voice sounded in her head and she realised they had stopped moving. She yanked open the door and stepped onto the cargo deck. Tenebrae's tank still dominated the space, her shining scales catching the portholes' light and casting weird purple shadows across the wooden walls. Laid out ten feet away, surrounded by crates and boxes, was a makeshift bed. Len was crouched over Epizon's prone form, and his head snapped up when Lyssa approached.

'Ah, you're here,' he said quietly. Lyssa looked at Epizon's face as she crouched down beside him.

'He's asleep,' she murmured.

'He's sedated. The treatment will work faster if he is unconscious. And he was very confused when he awoke just after you left.'

'Confused?' Lyssa frowned at the satyr.

'Yeah. Kept talking about going to Virgo.'

'Virgo?' asked Phyleus, and Lyssa was sure there was slight panic in his voice.

'Yeah. He wasn't really talking sense, though. We'll wake him up in a few hours.' Len laid his hand on Lyssa's shoulder. 'I'm really, really glad I'm still here, Captain,' he said quietly.

Lyssa smiled warmly at him. 'I'd have got you back if he'd taken you,' she said.

'But then I wouldn't be immortal, like you lot.' Len grinned.

'You know, we actually have to win Trials to become immortal,' she drawled.

'We're joint winners! Two wins each, for us, the giants and...' he trailed off instead of saying Hercules's name.

'Yeah,' Lyssa said, watching Epizon's chest rise and fall gently. They all fell quiet.

'How's your arm?' Len asked eventually.

'Numb, mostly. Painful if I move fast.'

'I'll go and make up some more ointment,' he replied, and picked up his small medical bag. 'He'll be right as rain in no time, Cap,' he said, then trotted towards the hauler.

'LEN's so different when he's working,' said Phyleus.

Lyssa looked at him. He was standing in front of Tenebrae's tank, watching her tail flick gently in the liquid. The creature's intense gaze was fixed on Epizon and it made Lyssa feel uneasy. She stood up, moving between Epizon and the tank, then sat down beside him, on the wooden planks.

'You were telling me something,' she said to Phyleus, drawing her knees up and resting her good elbow on them.

'Yes. I was.' He sat down too, leaning his back against the tank. 'I knew which way to go to get the gem. This is going to sound strange, so...' He trailed off.

'Phyleus, look around you. I'm used to strange,' she said impatiently.

'I guess. I've never told anybody this,' he said, pushing his hand through his hair. 'How much do you know about Virgo?' Lyssa's eyebrows drew together.

'As much as anyone knows. Hardly anything,' she answered.

'There's a test, held on Virgo every year. It's called the Elysium Mysteries. The gods invite powerful families to take part, and they are sworn to secrecy. No doubt your family would have been asked if... You know.'

Lyssa looked at her hands.

'Yeah. I know.'

'Most turn the invitation down, because very few survive the Mysteries. My father accepted it.'

Lyssa looked up at him.

'He sent you,' she said quietly. Phyleus nodded.

'My mother cried for a week before the test, but she didn't stop him or speak out against him. There was a ceremony on Taurus, where my family as good as said goodbye to me, then I was taken to Virgo. I was blindfolded and given wine to drink that makes the stuff Dionysus brews seem like water. It induces madness so brutal that most people kill themselves. Thankfully, I can't remember anything I saw. One of the perks of surviving. My skin was shredded when I came around and all of my fingers and toes were broken, but the hallucinations and all memory of them were gone.'

Lyssa's stomach turned.

'Why? Why would your father put you through that?' she whispered.

'The rewards if you survive,' Phyleus said, meeting her eyes. 'My injuries were healed instantly and I was made stronger than I was before. Those who survive the Mysteries are given power.'

'Given power? On Virgo? You don't mean...' Lyssa stared at him. 'Power from *Hades*?'

Phyleus nodded and her mouth fell open.

'Nothing too epic,' he said, his mouth quirking in a smile. 'I can't talk to the dead or turn invisible. Sadly.'

'What can you do?'

'I can sense precious metals and stones,' he said. 'Hades was god of the underworld in ancient Olympus, living underground, and has an affinity with gifts of the earth.'

'So you knew which way the sapphire was,' Lyssa said, understanding.

'Yeah. Also...' He bit his lip.

'What?'

'Erm, this is going to sound a bit morbid, but... I know when someone is about to die.'

Lyssa gaped, then leaped to her feet.

'How the hell have you not mentioned this already?' she exploded. 'You knew this whole time that Epizon would be OK?'

Phyleus scrambled to his feet, waving his hands.

'No! No, no, I only know right before it's about to happen, it's a mostly useless power!' he insisted, stepping towards her. 'Honestly, the only time it's ever been useful was when we were on Sagittarius.'

'What?'

'When we were flying through the spikes on the long-boat. I didn't stop you because I knew that if we were about to die then I would know.'

Irrational emotion fired inside her.

'So you didn't let me carry on just because you believed in me?' she said, before she could stop herself. Phyleus blinked.

'I believe in you now,' he said quietly.

She hissed and turned away, sitting back down hard and cursing herself mentally. Why had she said that?

'It's true, Lyssa. I told you, I can help you. And we have more in common than you thought.'

He was right. On both counts. A boy sent to endure lethal, torturous madness by his own father, strong enough to survive and endowed with the power of Hades. How had her judgement of him been so wrong?

HERCULES

Hercules stared at the flame dish, without seeing the orange flickers dancing across the metal. Ati was sitting on his lap, and he ran his fingers over her smooth, hairless skin. There was a vivid scene playing out in his mind.

He was standing in Zeus's throne room, gleaming white marble under his feet and the walls and ceiling open to the glittering, swirling skies. He could see the mansions of Leo in the distance, nestled in the thick grey cloud that circled the towering mountaintop where he stood. Zeus beamed at him from his throne, and the other gods bent their heads deferentially. Hedone, standing beside him, ran a silken soft finger down his arm.

'I pronounce you, Hercules, the winner of the Immortality Trials,' his father boomed, purple lightning flashing around them in celebration. Hercules shivered as he imagined the moment. What would ichor would actually *feel* like, running through his own veins, fuelling endless life?

. . .

'CAPTAIN?' asked a quiet voice, snapping him from his vision. 'Can I get you anything?' He looked up from the flames at Evadne. She had her head bowed and her hands clasped together meekly. Her subservience stirred his desires, but he called Hedone's beautiful face to his mind. He would not share his bed with Evadne. Not any more.

'Wine,' he grunted.

'Of course,' she said and turned to go, but the flame dish sparked to life. The flames leaped white, then faded, leaving the image of the Trial announcer, perky and beaming. Hercules ground his teeth.

'Good day, Olympus! It was a shame to say goodbye to one of our competitors today, but what a reward for the *Orion!* And now, a reward for all of you.' He winked as he dropped his voice conspiratorially. 'The heroes of the Trials have a very exclusive invitation... To a feast thrown by none other than the goddess of love herself! Tomorrow night, the heroes will all attend Aphrodite's palace on Pisces, where they will feast, drink and dance, before finding out what they must do for their next Trial. Enjoy!' he sang, then vanished from the flames.

Hercules narrowed his eyes at the flame dish, annoyed. Another feast on Pisces. He had attended hundreds, and he didn't feel like feasting. He felt like... like winning. Like fighting and winning. Unspent rage and power roiled through him and he looked up at Evadne again.

'I'll get your wine,' she said quickly, and scurried towards the hauler. Power pulsed through him and he shifted restlessly. Pisces was a long way off, hundreds of leagues, and it would take more than a day to get there. He directed the ship east with his mind, feeling the slight pull under him as she changed direction. He stroked Ati again and took a long breath in. At least the feast would give him time with Hedone. He was desperate to see her. And when he did, he would make sure that the wait had been worth it.

'What did you do with the gems?' Eryx asked Busiris over his mug of ale.

'Wouldn't you like to know.' The half-giant smiled back at him.

'We all get a share!' Eryx exclaimed, banging the tankard down on the galley table.

'I have the gems,' boomed Antaeus across them both. At the other end of the massive table, the brothers Albion and Bergion stopped arguing and looked over. 'They stay on the ship until the end of the Trials, then they will be shared out.'

'What if we don't survive until the end of the Trials?' asked Albion. Busiris snorted.

'Then you won't care if you miss your share,' he sneered.

'What if I want mine now?' Bergion said, standing up and glowering at Busiris.

'You won't have a chance to spend them,' pointed out Eryx, taking a long drag of his drink.

'At a party on Pisces? There'll be plenty of women interested in a couple of rubies,' answered Bergion, his eyes lighting up as he spoke. He was right, realised Eryx. Everybody looked at Antaeus.

'Fine. One gem each,' the captain sighed. The brothers cheered and clanked their mugs together, then downed the contents. Eryx smiled.

'What a waste,' Busiris muttered.

'What is?'

'Giving those idiots gems to spend on women.'

'And what would you spend yours on?' asked Eryx.

'Mine will be replacing what I spent on this ship,' he answered haughtily. Eryx rolled his eyes. Busiris never missed a chance to remind them that he paid for the *Orion*.

'So you'll be all by yourself on Pisces?'

'No. I just won't be paying for it,' Busiris answered. 'You forget, Eryx, that I'm royalty. The king of Egypt does not need to pay for company.'

Eryx snorted.

'Nobody has even heard of Egypt. Giants don't get human women for free, even on Pisces.'

Busiris glared at him.

'Of course they've heard of Egypt. Just because you're untravelled and ill-educated doesn't mean Aphrodite's courtesans are,' he snapped.

'I'm travelling now,' shot back Eryx. 'How many folk will be able to say they've seen all twelve realms? At the end of all this, I'll be one of the best-travelled citizens in all of Olympus!'

Antaeus laughed.

'Eryx is right, Busiris,' he said, smiling.

The gold-skinned half-giant narrowed his eyes and stood up. 'I'm going to read,' he said, and stalked out of the galley. The brothers ignored him as he passed, rolling dice and arguing.

'Why did you make him your first mate?' asked Eryx, feeling bold after the ale.

'He paid for the *Orion*,' sighed Antaeus. 'He's not so bad, Brother.'

Eryx frowned. 'He thinks he's better than us.'

'He *is*. He's royalty. And he won the last Trial for us.'

'Hmmm,' said Eryx. He knew he shouldn't push Busiris. He wasn't sure why the black-eyed half-giant hadn't already told Antaeus about Evadne's visits. But nor could Eryx control how much he disliked him.

4

EVADNE

Evadne rolled over in bed with a sigh. Maybe she should read a bit more, she thought. It was better than just lying there, unable to sleep. But she'd read all the books in her own room. She would have to sneak into Hercules's quarters to get more.

She screwed up her face at the thought. Once, she'd been in his rooms all the time, able to get out of his bed, sit on his armchair and read his books as much as she pleased. What had changed?

Hedone, she thought, frustration welling inside her. Hedone was the reason she was no longer welcome in his bedroom. She would never have guessed that he would want to be loyal to one woman. But then again... Hedone was no ordinary woman. If they were serious about a relationship, then Hedone would have to join the crew of the *Hybris*. And then Evadne would be even less important.

She sat up in bed, pushing her hair out of her face. She needed to prove she was useful. Hercules still had every chance of winning immortality and she needed to be part of his crew when he did.

A flash of doubt struggled to the surface of her thoughts. *What if he keeps losing? You may not survive until the end of the Trials.* She rubbed her bare arms. She had a back-up plan. Eryx would help her, if she needed it. But right now she needed a plan to keep Hercules happy. To keep her relevant. She needed to turn the tables, to make sure they could win more Trials.

SHE PUSHED THE SHEETS AWAY, and swung her legs off the bed. Somewhere she had a book by Athena, about competitive strategy. Maybe she could get some inspiration from that.

Evadne walked silently across the room and scanned the bookshelf in the dim light from her porthole, until she found the book she was after.

The problem was, Hercules was unpredictable. She knew now that he had a bloodlust. A desire to kill that made him dangerous. But unless there were more Trials with beasts to slay, that wouldn't help them. She needed to be smarter. She needed help.

5

LYSSA

'Epizon?' Lyssa whispered.

His eyes fluttered open, his pupils expanding quickly in the dim light of the cargo deck.

'Captain?' he croaked.

She beamed at him.

'Yes, Ep. I'm here.'

His peaceful face contorted quickly and he tried to sit up. 'Whoa,' she said, pushing him gently back down. 'You shouldn't be sitting up yet.'

'But Captain, we can't go to Virgo,' he said, his voice frantic. She frowned as she leaned over him.

'We're not, Ep, don't worry. We're going nowhere near Virgo.'

He relaxed back into the makeshift bed.

'Good. We can't. Ever.' His dark eyes fixed on hers.

'Why?'

He opened his mouth to answer but confusion crossed his face.

'I don't know,' he said eventually.

Lyssa raised her eyebrows. She decided not to point out

that they would have to go when Hades' Trial was announced.

'How are you feeling?' she asked him instead.

'Awful,' he answered, closing his eyes. 'Len said the crew gave blood to save me.'

'Yep. You have some of Abderos's and...' She trailed off, thinking about what Phyleus had just told her. Did he have ichor in his blood? Did that mean Epizon did now?

'Phyleus,' Epizon finished for her. 'You're struggling to say his name now?'

'No, sorry, I just... You were right,' she said. Epizon opened one eye. 'There's more to him than I realised. And he does deserve a place on the *Alastor*.'

He gave her a small smile.

'I'm glad to hear it. How did the Trial go?'

'Er, we came second,' she answered, as he closed his eyes again.

'Second?'

'Yeah. So not great.'

'How's your shoulder?'

'Good. Really good. I don't need the sling any more. I haven't tried to do any heavy lifting yet, but... Len's potions work magic.'

Epizon grunted.

'Where are we going now?' he asked.

'Pisces. I need your help.'

'I'm in no state to help anybody, Captain.'

'I need your advice,' she said awkwardly.

'Ah. OK, I'll do my best.'

'Thanks. Keep your eyes closed, though, it's easier.'

Epizon smiled widely this time.

'I see. Let me guess... Your feelings for Phyleus are

getting stronger and you're about to go to the realm of love and you're worried they'll get the better of you.'

'You've been to Pisces, you know what it's like!' Lyssa wailed. 'Even people you don't fancy that much become gorgeous.'

'Lyssa, if you like him, just enjoy the feeling! Go with it. See what happens.'

'I can't,' she grumbled.

'Why not?'

'Lots of reasons.' She held up her hand and ticked them off her fingers as she spoke. 'One, I can't be distracted by anything at the moment; the Trials are the most important thing. Two, he's a prince, and seriously, can you see me with a prince? Three, while I'm admitting that there's something there, he still irritates the hell out of me. Four.' Lyssa dropped her voice to a whisper and closed her own eyes. 'I'm worried about controlling my power.'

'What do you mean?'

'I've been getting... strong surges of power around him.'

'Rage?'

Lyssa shook her head, feeling her cheeks heat.

'Yes, but not from anger.'

'Oh. Oh, I see. Has that happened before?'

'A little, but not like this.'

They both fell silent.

'Well, the first three reasons aren't really issues at all,' Epizon said eventually. He carried on, cutting off her noise of protest, 'He won't distract you, he'll ground you. He's renounced being a prince and the fact that he irritates you is what draws you to him.'

Lyssa huffed, scowling.

'Your power, though, I don't know. Do you think you would hurt someone? Hurt him?'

'I don't think so,' she said uncertainly. 'I'm more worried about sending the ship off a hundred leagues high.'

Epizon laughed, wincing.

'Then don't get close to him on the *Alastor*.'

'I live on the *Alastor*,' she protested.

'You wanted my advice, here it is. Stop worrying about it. See what happens on Pisces, enjoy it. Keep control of your emotions and your power as best you can. Trust him to help you.'

'Really?'

'Lyssa, you knew this was what I would say. You've come to me to be told that it's OK.' She sighed. He was right. She hadn't thought for a minute he would tell her to avoid Phyleus.

'Thanks, Epizon,' she said, and leaned over to kiss his cheek. He smiled. 'I'm really, really glad you're OK.'

'Me too, Captain. Now let me sleep.'

6

HEDONE

Hedone twirled in front of the full-length mirror in her room, watching the crimson red dress shimmer as it moved. Evadne had looked good in the colour at the feast on Taurus but Hedone saved red for very special occasions.

Tied at her neck, the chiffon fabric of the dress cascaded down her chest in two sections, covering her breasts but leaving her navel exposed. A black ribbon of sparkling crystals wrapped low around her hips, joining the chiffon to a slinky, flowing skirt. Her dark hair fell down her bare back, loose strands accentuating her elegant neck and throat.

She hoped Hercules would be impressed. She was desperate to see him. The two-day journey to Pisces had felt like a lifetime to her, waiting and wanting him so badly. She'd thought she might die when Hermes announced somebody was leaving; the wait to find out if she would be removed was unbearable. Her heart had been pounding so hard, her breathing so shallow, that she had become faint.

Now she squeezed her eyes shut, sending thanks to Hermes for the hundredth time that she had stayed.

Hercules wouldn't want her if she wasn't immortal with him. He would outlive her, and move on to somebody else. The thought made her feel sick. She opened her eyes and looked in the mirror once more.

She didn't need to think like that. She would be seeing him soon. And it would be worth the wait. They would dance and drink and laugh and she would get a glimpse of life after the Trials. A life with him. Thrills ran through her and goosebumps rose on her arms. She had found love. She knew this was it. Real, true love.

THESEUS LOOKED EFFORTLESSLY CHARMING, his brown hair tied back with braids and an easy smile on his face as he leaned against the top-deck railings.

'Wow,' he said, as Hedone stepped out of the hauler and onto the deck of the *Virtus*.

She smiled.

'You look great too, Captain,' she said. He was wearing a traditional silver toga, tied with black cord, which made his warm brown skin seem to glow. The uneasy wrenching feeling Hedone had been experiencing lasted only a second, and then Psyche appeared, holding a tray of wine glasses.

'Drink before we go?' she said. Hedone smiled and took a glass. Psyche was in silver too, a dress cut high at the front but as low as it could get at the back, with no sleeves and a long split up the right leg. It sparkled when she moved.

'That's a great dress, Psyche,' Hedone said.

'Thanks,' the woman replied indifferently. 'To Bellerephon,' she said, raising her glass.

'To Bellerephon,' they chanted back, taking a sip. Bellerephon had been disappointed, of course, and Theseus had been as close to angry as he got, but Hedone suspected that Psyche wasn't overly bothered by his loss.

'There's Pisces,' said Theseus, turning to look out over the railings. They were flying low over the glittering ocean, and the tropical island paradise was growing larger in the distance. Pinks and purples rolled through the sky around them, and a warm breeze whispered over Hedone's skin. She'd missed her home.

7

LYSSA

'I got you a present,' said Phyleus, as Lyssa opened her cabin door a crack.

'What?'

'I got you a present,' he repeated, slouching casually against the wood-panelled wall outside her door.

'Why?'

'That's not what you're supposed to say,' he said, rolling his eyes. 'You're supposed to say *Why, thank you, Phyleus, you're so kind. However can I repay you?*' He grinned at her.

'Not a chance,' she said, scowling. 'Why aren't you dressed yet?' He was supposed to be in a toga for the feast, as tradition stated, but he was still wearing his normal clothes.

'Because I wanted to give you this first,' he said, his brown eyes shining as he held out a flat box. Lyssa snaked one arm around the barely open door and took it hesitantly. It was heavier than it looked.

'Why are you hiding behind the door?' Phyleus asked her, his mouth quirking in a curious smile.

'I'm not,' she said, too quickly.

She was. And she was hiding because she was wearing the dress again. The gold one Dionysus had fabricated out of nothing for her, that fit like a glove, and, truth be told, was the only dress she had.

'Course you're not,' Phyleus said, pushing himself off the wall. 'I'll leave you to it, then.' He threw her one last grin and sauntered up the corridor, towards his and Abderos's room.

LYSSA SIGHED as she closed the door behind her and leaned against it. He'd already seen her in the dress. What was she hiding from? When had she ever been insecure about what she looked like?

Cross with herself, she realised she should have squashed her feelings. She needed to be stronger than this... really, she *was* stronger than this. Shaking her head a little, the equivalent of a mental slap, she carried the box over to her bed.

OPENING IT, Lyssa stared down at the most beautiful piece of jewellery she had ever seen. Her mouth hung open slightly as she took in the circlet, made of palest gold, and fashioned like a wreath, delicate leaves entwining together to form a circlet. Sprinkled throughout, at the base of the leaves, were deep blue stones, with shots of glittering gold catching and reflecting the light. Lapis Lazuli.

'Where did you get it?' she sent the thought to Phyleus immediately. 'We've not stopped anywhere; where did you find it?'

'People usually start with thank you.' His voice sounded in her head.

'Sorry, I'm sorry. Thank you. It's... Where did you get it?'

There was silence for a minute, then, 'It's been on board since we left Libra.'

Lyssa frowned.

'You bought this for me in Libra? You... You didn't like me before we left.' She stared, confused, at the circlet.

'I didn't buy it. It was my mother's.'

Lyssa's breath hitched.

'And if you remember, it was you who didn't like me. I told you we could be friends right from the start.'

'I can't accept this, Phyleus. Not if it belongs to your family.'

'I don't like my family,' he said, and she could picture him shrugging, his eyes sparkling with that defiance he wore so well.

'But...' she said, not knowing what to say next.

'Do you like it?' His voice was quiet in her head.

'Yes,' she whispered. 'It's stunning.'

'Then wear it tonight. Decide if you want to keep it later,' he said. She thought she could hear relief in his voice.

'I... I guess that's fair. Thank you,' she said, projecting her sincerity into the words the best she could.

'You're welcome, Captain.'

LYSSA TRIED to suppress the ripple of nerves as she stepped out of the hauler and onto the deck of the *Alastor*. Though the circlet nestled into her red curls weighed almost nothing, she was distinctly aware of it.

'Cap!' exclaimed Abderos, rolling across the deck towards her. 'You look... Wow!' He beamed up at her.

'You sure do, Captain.' Mischief sparkled in Len's eyes as he trotted up beside Abderos's chair. They were both wearing white togas, the satyr's draped open across his furry chest, which was far wider than Abderos's.

'You both look very smart too,' she said, scanning the deck.

'Looking for anyone in particular?' asked Abderos mildly. She snapped her eyes to his, a warning look on her face. Abderos threw up his hands in defence. 'I share a room with him! He's excited about tonight,' he said. 'I assumed the feeling was mutual.'

Lyssa could see the question in his face and turned away.

'The longboat will be here to pick us up in a minute; where is everyone?' she said evasively.

A clopping sounded and Nestor appeared from the other end of the deck. She too had a shining circlet atop her sleek white hair, and her armour gleamed. She nodded at Lyssa as she approached and Lyssa nodded back.

'Will Epizon be able to join us?' the centaur asked.

'No.' Len shook his head. 'He won't be up and about for another day or so.'

'I envy him. I abhor this celebrating,' Nestor said.

'You don't have to come, you know.' The satyr scowled.

Her tail flicked.

'I am a member of this crew and must represent it. Even in the seedy world of Aphrodite.'

'We're very close to the goddess herself to be saying such things,' Lyssa warned, glancing towards the island of Pisces beyond the ship railings.

The centaur snorted.

'I have the protection of the chaste Artemis. I do not fear the goddess of love.'

'I'm terrified of her,' said Phyleus, and Lyssa spun around.

He was wearing a black toga, belted with a shining silver strap, and his hair was damp and pushed back from his face. He stopped still as his eyes met hers, then slowly took her in. She did the same, her eyes catching on the bare skin of his chest.

'Are you wearing your boots?' he asked her.

Heat filled her cheeks. The dress was long, but not quite long enough to hide her feet.

'I don't have any other shoes,' she said fiercely. 'I only have this dress because Dionysus made it.'

'I like it. You could start a new trend.' He grinned, and sauntered over to the group. She huffed and turned to the railings. Where was this longboat?

'YOU LOOK INCREDIBLE.' His voice sounded in her head. 'You should keep the crown.'

This was more like it, Evadne thought, bringing her glass to her lips. Was this what Theseus's crew did all the time?

The feast hall was like nothing she had ever seen in her life. Like nothing she had ever dreamed of, even. It took up the half of Aphrodite's palace that faced the ocean and was completely open to the incredible view. Steps ran down from the hall to the sandy beach, waves lapping gently at the shore. There was no roof on the hall and the dimming orange skies twinkled above Evadne's head. Grand columns topped with flickering flames rose from the shining marble floor in a ring around a crystal-clear pool in the middle of the room. Luscious green palms twined up the columns and lined the outskirts of the huge room. Small round chest-height marble tables dotted the room, where people were putting down their drinks and food and standing in clusters, talking and laughing. There were nymphs and dryads with trays everywhere, serving drinks and delicacies to the guests, wearing very little, and oozing allure. Evadne eyed a red-haired tree nymph a few feet from the column she was leaning against. Hercules had a thing for redheads. Well, he'd used to. Now, he only had eyes for Hedone. She hadn't seen her captain since they arrived, and she couldn't see the demi-goddess of pleasure either. It seemed so obvious to her that they were together. Had Theseus not realised?

She scanned the room for him, spotting him surrounded by admirers, male and female, human and creature alike. His braids were tied back from his face and she could see his beaming smile clearly. He was beautiful. Evadne sighed. There was no point telling Theseus that. He would have no time for her.

'I saw you.'

Evadne whirled around at the voice, almost spilling her drink. Busiris was standing almost out of sight, by a pillar. She scowled and faced him.

'You made me jump,' she snapped.

'I saw you, when you came to the *Orion*.' His onyx eyes bored into hers and she looked away.

'I don't know what you're talking about,' she said, sipping her wine.

'Eryx is an idiot. You know that?'

She shrugged.

'I've got nothing to do with your ship, and I don't know or care whether Eryx is an idiot,' she answered coolly.

'I don't know what game you're playing, girl, but you can stop playing it with him,' the half-giant hissed.

'You're so sweet to look out for him.' She smiled sarcastically. Busiris snorted.

'I don't care about *him*. I care about winning.'

Evadne's face twitched as she suppressed the flash of triumph she felt. This could be just what she needed.

'Look, Busiris,' she said slowly. 'You know the *Orion* can't win.'

His face darkened.

'Of course—'

She cut him off.

'But Hercules... He can. Immortality is as good as ours, and you know it. Have you considered that you may be on the wrong crew?'

Busiris stared at her.

'What are you saying?'

'I'm saying that, when the time comes, you should think carefully about where your allegiances lie.'

'Has... Has Hercules said anything? About me?' Busiris's voice was hushed, excitement dancing across the words.

'He's hinted,' lied Evadne.

'But he didn't help me. On Capricorn, with the boar...' Busiris frowned. 'You were the only crew who would have left me to die.'

Evadne tutted.

'Don't be so stupid. It was clear the others would rescue you, so he thought it was better to stay out of their way and maintain his image and reputation for fierceness. He knew you wouldn't die.' She rolled her eyes and took another sip from her drink.

Busiris shifted his weight. He wasn't wearing a toga, but a knee-length white wrap that was tied with a bright red ribbon at his waist. His chest was bare and Evadne found herself wanting to touch his gold skin, wondering what it felt like. Bloody Aphrodite, she thought. Any little curiosity, any remote interest was heightened in this place.

'Why aren't you wearing a toga?' she asked him.

'This is what Egyptians wear,' he said proudly.

'The black lines around your eyes, are they Egyptian too?'

'Yes. We don't like to look like the rest of Aries' tribes.'

'Well, you definitely stand out,' she said. 'When the time comes, you'll know.' She didn't give him a chance to reply, but dropped her empty glass onto the tray of a passing nymph and sashayed off, towards the beach side of the hall.

That should keep him guessing. And keep him off Eryx's back too.

9

ERYX

Eryx watched as Evadne walked past the glittering pool. She was wearing a short dress, the same colour as her blue-black hair. It was impossible not to notice the shape of her body under the fabric. Why had she been talking to Busiris? Anxiety and not a little jealousy clouded his mind. She played games. He knew she would try to manipulate anybody into helping her. What had he expected?

She took a tall thin glass of sparkling liquid from a server and leaned against a palm tree, looking out over the ocean waves. He took a step towards her before he could stop himself. He needed to know what they had been talking about. Was Busiris warning her off him? Or had she played them both, telling Busiris all the same things she had told him? Had she played dice with him?

He had to know. He strode towards her, before he could lose his nerve.

'Eryx.' She smiled at him as he reached her. 'You don't have a drink.'

'I don't like wine,' he said, dimly aware that this wasn't how he'd planned to open the conversation.

'Just ask for something else, then.'

'No, I...' he started, but she blinked up at him and he forgot what he'd been about to say. She was beautiful. No matter how hard he fought it, the fact remained that he found her entrancing. 'I wanted to know why you were talking to Busiris,' he forced out. Her face darkened.

'That's none of your business.' She turned back to the waves.

'It is my business! He's on my crew. And he doesn't like me.'

'Yeah, I got that impression. Are you jealous?'

The playful tone of her voice angered him immediately.

'Don't toy with me. You should stay away from him, Evadne. I don't trust him,' he growled.

'Well, at least you've got something right,' she muttered, and sipped her drink.

'What do mean?'

'Why don't you trust him, Eryx?' she looked at him, eyebrows raised, waiting for his answer.

'I... I... I just don't. He's shifty. He's a coward.'

Evadne rolled her eyes.

'He's smart and he's driven,' she said.

'You're defending him?'

'No! I'm saying those are the two reasons you shouldn't trust him.'

Eryx drew his eyebrows together.

'You're smart,' he said quietly.

'Yeah. And I'm driven,' she replied, looking back down at her drink.

'So I shouldn't trust you either?'

She turned to him and the frustration on her face caught him by surprise.

'Eryx, you're a fool.' He scowled and folded his massive arms and Evadne let out a long breath. 'Of course you shouldn't trust me.'

He stared at her for a long moment, her words forcing him to admit what he didn't want to believe.

'You sabotaged the longboat. On Sagittarius,' he said eventually.

She nodded. Anger spiked in him.

'They could have been killed,' he hissed.

Evadne looked into her drink again.

'The prize is worth it,' she whispered.

Eryx took a step back from her.

'You would shorten others' lives to extend your own?'

'That's what these Trials are!' she answered fiercely. 'That's what everyone is doing!'

'No.' Eryx shook his head. 'No, they're risking their own lives, and making their own decisions. The only hero who has attacked another is *your captain*.' He spat the last words. 'I saw what he did to Captain Lyssa under the water on Scorpio. He wasn't trying to win the Trial. He was trying to kill his own daughter.'

Evadne said nothing and Eryx suddenly felt sick. She didn't care. He'd hoped that she was better than Hercules. That she was under his influence, scared or confused; but looking at her now, defiant and cold, he knew that wasn't true.

'You could have killed my captain. If you're so driven by winning that you can justify murder, then you're on your own, Evadne,' he said quietly, his gut twisting as he turned and walked away from her.

10

HERCULES

'So what about your parents?' asked Hedone.

'My adopted parents were kind enough, but simple,' Hercules answered with a shrug as he strolled along the fine sand, swinging Hedone's shoes in his right hand. His left gripped hers.

As soon as he had seen her in that dress, his brain had been unable to process anything. She'd slipped from the feast hall moments after arriving, and he had followed her. She'd led him through the palace to a bedroom, covered in red drapes and cushions. Aphrodite's palace was filled with such rooms, prefect for private trysts, and they had been left completely undisturbed.

His desire sated for the time being, they walked along the beach, holding hands because nobody else was around. Though Hercules was ceasing to care whether Theseus knew of his feelings for Hedone. He still didn't want to force a confrontation with the man, not yet, but he couldn't not be with her. Her body, her voice, her lips, her scent, they were all intoxicating.

'I never met my parents,' she said, kicking lightly at the sand. 'They left me at the temple when I was born, and Theseus brought me to Pisces when I was sixteen.'

'They knew you would be powerful,' Hercules told her, lifting her hand to his mouth and kissing the back of it. She smiled at him, and his whole body reacted.

'You think I'm powerful?'

'Very.'

She looked thoughtful.

'Do you think I am strong?'

Hercules thought for a moment, before answering.

'I think you are strong of mind.'

She laughed, a twinkling laugh.

'Not simple like your parents, then?'

'No, no, definitely not,' he smiled.

'Would you...' Hedone trailed off, looking back at her feet nervously.

'Go on.' Hercules gave her hand a squeeze of encouragement.

'Would you ever be able to have children again? After what Hera made you do?' Hedone looked at him hopefully, from under her thick lashes.

Children? He hadn't ever considered having more children. If he were to be immortal, what would be the point? But he could see the answer Hedone wanted, clear on her face. And how could he deny her anything?

'Of course. In time,' he said.

She beamed and squeezed his hand.

'We should get back,' she said, looking over her shoulder at the palace, the white marble dazzling against the deep pink sky and the bright blue ocean. 'Aphrodite will be arriving soon.'

Hercules nodded, and stopped walking. He spun her close to him, shuddering with pleasure at her giggle.

'Kiss me, my goddess,' he whispered.

'Always,' she breathed back, as her lips met his.

Aphrodite showed off her flawless beauty by being naked save for a thin, silk robe that covered her enticing parts. A curious breath of air would suddenly, and excitedly blow the robe aside, revealing her virgin bloom. Then it would blow directly on the garment, causing it to cling to her, clearly outlining the pleasing promise of her body. Aphrodite's appearance gave contrasting colours to the viewer, her skin shining white and her robe a dark blue like the sea she was born from.

EXCERPT FROM

The Golden Ass by Apuleius

Written 2 AD

Paraphrased by Eliza Raine

11

LYSSA

‘Y ou really love strawberries, huh?’ Phyleus smiled at Lyssa as she picked a plump red fruit from a passing tray.

‘Yup,’ she said, dropping the strawberry into her mouth and closing her eyes.

‘They're not my favourite,’ said Abderos. ‘I like oranges.’

Phyleus pulled a face.

‘Oranges? Over strawberries? No way,’ he said, shaking his head.

A loud gong sounded, interrupting the impending argument.

‘Please, honoured guests, welcome your host.’ A low seductive voice echoed through the hall. The room stilled, guests turning their heads this way and that, in search of the goddess. Lyssa looked around too. She had seen everyone from the Trials except Hercules, along with a number of famous faces, but no gods. All the beautiful nobodies desperately trying to be somebodies made her uncomfortable, so she had stuck like glue to her crew-mates. And every time Abderos had tried to wheel his way over to somebody else she had either found a reason for him to stay or gone with him, so that she would not be alone with Phyleus.

SHE REALISED people were pointing at the pool, hands to their gasping mouths, and she craned her neck to look. Rising from the water, bone-dry and breath-taking, was Aphrodite. She was wearing a gossamer robe of deep, royal blue, draped effortlessly over one shoulder and tied at her waist. It was so sheer it covered none of her modesty and Lyssa cursed herself for blushing. She glanced sideways at Phyleus's gaping face and narrowed her eyes. White-blond hair the colour of Nestor's tumbled over Aphrodite's bare shoulder, shining with its own light, and ruby red lips stood out on her alabaster skin.

'Good evening, honoured guests,' she said, spreading her hands. 'Thank you so much for joining me.'

Lyssa's jaw twitched. Like they had a choice.

'Tonight we welcome the heroes of the Immortality Trials, as they stand on the brink of taking on their eighth Trial.' She stepped gracefully across the surface of the pool and accepted a glass of sparkling liquid from a waiting dryad. She raised it in the air. 'To the noble heroes,' she said.

'To the noble heroes,' the room echoed, everyone raising their glasses in a toast. Lyssa didn't drink. She scanned the hall, looking for Hercules, but she couldn't see him. He would be loving this, she thought darkly.

'So we have the *Alastor*, the *Hybris* and the *Orion* with two wins each, and the *Virtus* with one. Hmmm. As much as I have enjoyed watching the Trials so far, I think Hermes let you off pretty easily.' She smiled. 'I'm going to add a little more... danger to the next one. But as always, with great risk comes great reward. The winner of the next Trial will be granted any wish they like.'

A murmur of excitement rippled through the room and Abderos looked up at Lyssa.

'Captain—' he started, but Aphrodite spoke again and he fell silent.

'The Trial will begin in one hour. Dance, drink, eat, love,' she said, her seductive voice spurring people's feet to move. Music began playing and Lyssa was swaying in time with it before she realised what she was doing.

'Captain! Captain, she said *any wish*!' Abderos's face was alive with excitement. Lyssa stilled, staring at him. 'My legs! This is it! I'm going to be able to walk again!'

'Ab...' She said slowly. 'We may not win.'

He dismissed her words with a wave of his hand.

'This is what I've been waiting for, Captain, a wish from the gods!'

'She said this one would be dangerous, Ab,' said Phyleus.

'So? They've all been dangerous. Captain, please, please use the wish on my legs?'

Lyssa looked into his eager young face, her chest tightening.

'Of course I will, if we win, but you can't get your hopes up like this. The goal is to stop Hercules from winning.'

A flicker of doubt passed over his face, but it was gone in an instant.

'You can win, Cap, I know you can.'

'I'm injured. Epizon is still out of action. We don't even know what the Trial is yet! Please, Ab, don't get too excited about this,' she pleaded.

'I know you'll do it,' he insisted.

Gods, she wanted to. Winning Abderos his wish would

be incredible. But the *Alastor* wasn't at full strength, they were on Theseus's home realm, and there were too many things they didn't know.

'I'll try, Abderos,' she said quietly. He beamed at her and she turned away, guilt washing through her.

'You will try, and we'll be here too,' said Phyleus, his voice in her head. She looked at him, drinking in the steady reassurance showed by the small nod he gave her. Nestor's hooves clicked on the marble as she approached them.

'Are you ready, Captain?' she asked.

'No,' said Lyssa, and downed the remainder of her wine. 'Aphrodite told us to dance, drink and eat. So that's what I'm going to do.'

'Excellent,' said Phyleus, and he followed her to where everyone was now dancing.

THE MUSIC WAS different to what she had heard on other realms. There was a slow, steady pulse under the melody, and keeping time with it was effortless, her body moving of its own accord to the beat. Phyleus caught her hand and spun her around, and she let him. Why not? Epizon had said go with it.

'Abderos doesn't understand the pressure he's putting on you,' Phyleus said, in her head. 'But don't let it affect you.'

'I don't want to think about it now,' she answered, closing her eyes and wishing the music was louder. It seemed to respond, the volume increasing and taking over her thoughts.

'You need to. The Trial is in less than an hour,' he cut across them.

She opened her eyes and glared at him.

'Don't tell me what to do, Phyleus.'

'I'm not! I'm trying to help,' he protested, still holding her hand.

'Then give me an hour off! An hour off from being everybody's captain, from making decisions that may kill my friends, from risking their lives. An hour off from thinking about facing him again!' She was shouting at him, aloud, but nobody noticed. The music was too loud, and they were all as caught up in the song as she wanted to be.

Phyleus stared at her for a heartbeat, then pulled her to him. Her body slammed into his, pain registered in her shoulder, and then his hand was in her hair, pulling her face towards his. Their lips met and desire erupted through her whole body. Her mind emptied, nothing but heat and longing and pleasure rippling through her in streams. She kissed him hungrily, pulling her hand free of his and finding his chest. She pressed her palm flat to his skin, feeling his heartbeat thudding against his ribs as his now-free hand wrapped around her waist.

'Gods, I want you,' he whispered, breaking the kiss and moving back to look at her. 'You're... You're incredible.'

Lyssa stared at him, panting slightly, her skin vibrating with power.

'Dance with me, Phyleus,' she said. 'For one hour, take me away.'

He leaned in, kissing her again, softly this time, and shivers flitted across her skin, nerves tingling.

'Anything for my captain,' he murmured, moving his hips against hers as the music beat through their bodies.

12

ERYX

E ryx leaned against a column, watching the waves
lap gently at the sand, the twilight sky beyond
reflected in its calm surface. How little like Scorpio's oceans it was, he thought. The beat of the music pulsed
through him, making his muscles tense and his brain feel
foggy. He was relieved when it abruptly stopped. Fighting
the urge to go and find Evadne was exhausting.

'Heroes,' sang Aphrodite's voice. He turned towards the
pool, where she was once again standing. He scanned the
throng of dancing bodies, and he saw Evadne, chest heaving, smiling at a barely dressed maenad. His breath hitched,
and he forced himself to concentrate on the goddess. Once
his eyes were on her, it wasn't hard to keep them there. She
was like every dream any man, or woman, didn't know they
had. All possible desires in one place. Her robe clung to her
perfect body and he swallowed hard.

'It is time for your eighth Trial. There are some stables
not far from here, run by the vicious Diomedes. He has four
horses that are quite exceptional in that they breathe fire.
They are also quite mad, for Diomedes has fed them since

birth on human flesh. Capture one of these horses, and you shall be the victor.' Aphrodite smiled a heart-warming smile, and suddenly Eryx was outside the palace.

He looked left and right. His crew were there, standing beside him in the dim light, the giants looming tall. They were on earthy ground, trees dotting the landscape. Far in the distance he could see firelight, and a low building.

'Is that the stables?' he asked, pointing.

'I guess so.' Antaeus shrugged, and lurched off towards them.

THEY WALKED QUICKLY, and the sky dimmed ever more dramatically the further from the palace they got. As they got closer the low building revealed itself to be a single-storey wooden hut.

'Didn't she say they breathed fire?' asked Busiris quietly.

'Yeah. Why?'

'I wouldn't keep anything that breathed fire in a building made from wood,' he answered.

Eryx thought about it. Busiris was right. That didn't make sense.

A distant neighing sounded, though, and Antaeus raised his eyebrows and kept walking. They slowed as they got close, straining to see or hear anything. There was a light flickering between the planks of the back of the building, a brazier perhaps. They crept closer, just a few feet from the hut, veering towards the left wall. Where were the other crews? Suddenly, bright flickering light framed the building, accompanied by a loud screech. Eryx ducked instinctively, but the light died down quickly, along with the eerie sound.

'What was that?' Antaeus hissed.

'The fire-breathing horses, I would imagine, Captain,' answered Busiris. Eryx glared at him.

'Keep moving,' Antaeus grunted. They edged their way around the building, the calm quiet of the place forcing silence upon them. When they reached the end of the building they all stopped, craning over each other to peer around the wood.

TETHERED to an enormous brazier in front of the hut were four giant white mares. They were so large Antaeus could easily have ridden one. Their coats gleamed in the firelight as they ducked their heads, feasting on something that lay on the ground. Eryx leaned forward to look, but he already knew what they were eating. He could smell the bloody tang of raw meat in the air. Albion let out a long breath beside him.

'They're beautiful,' whispered Antaeus.

One of the horses raised its head, snickering at another as it tore a large chunk of meat off the carcass and lifted it high. The first horse bared its teeth and Eryx saw that its eyes were as solid and black as Busiris's were. A light in the creature's mouth caught his attention, and he jumped as the horse roared flames at the beast with the meat. The blaze shot forward at least six feet and the other mare leaped backwards, kicking and snarling. The mares continued to scrap with each other, the meat becoming charred as they fought over it. Eryx dropped to a crouch.

How in the name of Zeus were they going to catch one of those things?

The eighth task Hercules had to complete was capturing the mares of Diomedes the Thracian. The troughs the horses fed from were made of brass because their teeth were so savage, and they were only kept in one place by strong iron chains. They did not eat natural produce of the earth like other horses, rather they fed on the flesh of strangers, tearing apart their limbs.

EXCERPT FROM

LIBRARY OF HISTORY BY DIODORUS SICULUS

Written 1 BC

Paraphrased by Eliza Raine

13

HEDONE

Hedone leaned against the tree and watched the horses as they fought, blasting shots of fire at one another and tossing meat between them. They were at the same time quite beautiful and incredibly ugly.

'Where's Diomedes?' whispered Psyche. 'And why do I have to do this in a damn dress? I thought we'd be sent back to the *Virtus* first or I'd have worn something different.'

Hedone cast a glance at Psyche's impressive dress, then looked down at her own open-fronted garment. She wasn't expecting to get close to those things, so she wasn't all that worried. She scanned the darkening plain, looking for signs of the other crews. For signs of Hercules.

'The giants are behind the stable,' murmured Theseus. She looked, and caught sight of movement, too high up to be human.

'The others?'

'I don't know.'

'Look!' One of the black-skinned giants was creeping around the side of the stable, towards the horses. Movement in the other direction caught Hedone's eye, and her heart skipped as she saw the distinctive outline of a lion-skin cloak, growing clearer as it got nearer to the firelight.

'Hercules,' growled Psyche.

The giant reached the mares first. Their snickering and scrapping stopped abruptly and they all turned to the huge man in unison. Their silver-white tails flicked back and forth and a high keening sound started.

Then there was an earth-shaking boom and Hedone gripped the tree involuntarily. There was another boom, and another, and the giant froze in place. Hercules kept moving, though, and she realised he was now only ten feet from the horses.

'Who visits me and my mares this night?' The deep voice rang through the air and Hedone's skin felt tight as anxiety prickled at her. The booms got louder as a man stepped out of the stable building. Not a man, she realised, as she watched. A giant. He grew as she stared, each booming step he took adding a foot to his height. By the time he reached the brazier, the horses bobbing their heads and moving aside for him, he was at least twenty feet tall.

He looked around slowly, catching sight of Albion.

'I asked who you were,' he cried.

'Albion,' the smaller giant grunted.

'Why are you here, Albion?'

The giant stared mutely up at him.

'You're not here to take my mares, are you?' roared the still-growing giant. 'You would dare to steal from me? The great Diomedes?' He threw his arms out as he bellowed, and Albion took a stumbling step backwards.

. . .

HEDONE COULDN'T KEEP her eyes on either Diomedes or
Albion. She was watching Hercules, who was still creeping
closer to the horses. He was only three feet away from them
now, and she watched with baited breath as he crouched
low, trying to go unnoticed. With a flick of its tail one of the
horses turned around and Hercules froze in place. The
horse moved its head slowly, then let out a screeching
whinny as it opened its mouth. Hercules threw his cloak up
over his face as the stream of fire engulfed his body and
Hedone cried out, taking half a step away from the tree
before Psyche grabbed her arm and yanked her back.

'What in Zeus's name are you doing?' the woman hissed
at her.

'Hercules!' Hedone whimpered, unable to see him
through the bright light of the fire. Diomedes began to
laugh, a huge, echoing sound, and the screeching stopped as
the jet of fire ebbed and died away. Hedone's hand went to
her mouth as she stared. Hercules wasn't there. She scanned
the landscape frantically, looking for him, and almost
collapsed when she saw a dark figure, moving fast and close
to the ground in the opposite direction. His cloak had
saved him.

'Leave!' bellowed Diomedes, and her attention snapped
back to the huge giant as all four mares turned to face
Albion, fire visible in their slowly opening mouths. Albion
ran, falling over his feet as he scrambled to get back behind
the stables, and Diomedes laughed again as the mares shot
their flames at his retreating figure.

NOBODY SAID anything as Diomedes walked back towards
the stables, shrinking as he approached them, his booming

footsteps steady and terrifying. As he disappeared inside, Psyche spun Hedone around to face her.

'What were you thinking?' she demanded, anger on her face.

'I...'

'She's in love with Hercules,' said Theseus. Psyche looked over her shoulder at him, her mouth falling open.

'That can't be true.' She turned back to Hedone. 'Is it?'

'Hera made him do it. Those things, years ago, it wasn't him,' she answered fiercely, pushing her chin out. 'He's a good man. A proud, strong man.'

'Hedone, he's a monster! He left Busiris to die on Capricorn, he tried to kill his own daughter on Scorpio—'

'*She* tried to kill him!' Hedone exclaimed. 'She's not the hero everyone thinks she is. She's... she's a tool of the gods. Just one more test for Hercules to overcome, before he can be at peace.' She turned away from Psyche, wishing the woman's incredulity didn't upset her so much. Why couldn't Psyche see Hercules as she could?

'Hedone, please, think about it, you know that's not true.' Psyche spoke softly and tears filled Hedone's eyes. She had so much respect for the woman. Since they had been training together, she had fallen for her abrupt manner and honest attitude. She admired her. But if Psyche wanted to come between her and Hercules, then their friendship was over.

'You're wrong,' she breathed, refusing to turn and look at her.

'Theseus, do something!' exploded Psyche.

'We need to win this Trial,' he said, 'then we'll talk about it.'

Psyche barked a noise of frustration.

'Fine. How do we win?' she snapped.

'We lure the horses somewhere they can't reach us. We need shovels, and we need to dig a trap.'

14

LYSSA

'Those horses are an abomination,' Nestor said, her severe face set and angry. 'Aphrodite should know better than to create such beings.'

'Any ideas on how to catch one?' asked Lyssa, her eyes fixed on the creatures. They were hiding in a small copse, barely large enough to conceal them all, about forty feet from the stable front.

'What do you think she means by *catch one*?' said Abderos. Lyssa looked at him. 'Like, does that mean, get a saddle on it and ride one? Or does it just mean incapacitate one for a minute or two?'

'That's actually a good question,' said Phyleus, looking at her. A pulse of lingering desire shot through her when his eyes met hers, and she shoved it away. She needed to concentrate.

'Let's assume the latter, and if that doesn't work try something else,' she said.

'So we need a net or something,' Abderos said.

'A net?' Len guffawed. 'They breathe fire, Ab. A net's not

going to last long. Unless it's made of metal...' He trailed off as he said it.

'The giants,' Lyssa breathed. They fashioned a giant metal net on Scorpio. If they got back to their ship... She looked to where the crew of the *Orion* had been hiding, behind the side of the stable, but they were no longer there. She scanned the sky, looking for longboats or anything moving, but just saw swirling purple clouds.

'Could we get their net?' Phyleus asked.

'From their ship? I... I guess we could try.'

'But, what if they get it first and then you're just wasting time searching the *Orion* for it?' Abderos sounded worried. 'Maybe we should wait for them to get it, then steal it from them here.'

'The giants are not clever,' said Nestor. 'They may not think to get it at all.'

'Busiris is,' Abderos said. 'I was in the cage with him on Capricorn and he's not like the others. He's smart.'

'None of this deals with Diomedes,' said Lyssa. 'Someone will need to distract him.' Everybody looked at her. She swallowed.

'He's not as big as a Hydra.' Phyleus shrugged. 'And you did all right with one of those.'

'We lost against the Hydra,' she growled at him. 'Half my boat got eaten and I nearly fell into a pit of flaming acid.'

'Then it's a good job there's no flaming acid this time.'

Lyssa closed her eyes.

'Right.'

'Cap, I don't think anybody except you could lift that net,' said Len thoughtfully.

'I can't fight Diomedes *and* throw the bloody net!' she exclaimed, throwing her hands in the air. 'Gods, I wish

Epizon was here,' she said under her breath, screwing up her face.

'I may be able to lift the net, said Nestor.

'With my help,' offered Phyleus.

'Fine. We don't even have the damn thing yet anyway. Len and I will go back to the palace and look for a longboat. We'll sneak on board the *Orion* and try to get the net. If they've already got it, we'll come straight back and steal it from them. Then I'll distract Diomedes and you two can catch a horse.'

'But, Cap...' started Abderos, but she continued speaking over him.

'Nestor, Phyleus, Abderos, stay here. Avoid Hercules at all costs. If he comes anywhere near any of you, run, don't fight. Do you understand?'

Phyleus nodded along with Nestor but she heard his voice clear in her head.

'I don't want to leave you.'

'I need you here, Phyleus.' She waited for him to argue, to tell her she was wrong, that he needed to be there to protect her.

'Yes, Captain.'

She blinked at him. Epizon's words swam through her mind. *Phyleus respects who you are. He doesn't want to challenge you. He just wants to prove himself to you.*

Epizon had been right, all this time.

15

HERCULES

Hercules crouched, snarling, as he flung off the burning-hot lion-skin cloak.

'Is it damaged?' asked Evadne quickly, leaning to inspect it.

'Of course not,' he barked. 'It's just hot. Asterion, these beasts are your kin, are they not?'

The minotaur shifted uncomfortably. He was hardly visible in the dim light, his fur blending into the dark, but his red eyes shone.

'Not exactly, Captain.'

'Can you communicate with them?'

'Yes, Captain, but it will not help. I'm sorry.'

'Why in Zeus's name not?' Hercules spat, fury rolling through his body. Those damn horses had made a fool of him, forcing him to run away.

'They are mad, Captain. All they do is repeat words.'

Evadne looked over at the snickering, screeching animals as she asked, 'What do they say?'

'*Blood*, mostly.'

Evadne shuddered and Hercules glared at them both.

'I need *Keravnos*.' He was furious with Aphrodite for sending them straight out on this Trial. Had he known, he would have brought the sword to the feast.

'Then we need to find a longboat,' Evadne muttered.

'Obviously,' he growled.

'Asterion, stay here. Watch the others. Do whatever it takes to stop them winning.' He turned to Evadne, who was hesitantly touching the cloak, testing the temperature. 'You stay too.'

She looked at him.

'Yes, Captain,' she said.

HE RAN BACK towards the palace, fast, his cloak firmly back around his shoulders. He needed this win. The competition was too tight, with too few Trials to go. He never would have dreamed that the others would do so well. They all had help from the gods, he thought, snarling. Aphrodite surely wouldn't dare help her favourite on her own Trial, though; it would be too obvious.

At the thought of Theseus, Hercules's mind slipped back to Hedone, and his legs pounded the earth harder, the palace growing larger. Soon. Soon she would move onto the *Hybris* with him, be with him forever.

He slowed as he reached a grand marble arch, signalling the entrance to the palace gardens. Somewhere there must be a longboat dock, he thought, scanning the twilight carefully. He jogged towards the closest out-building he could see.

As he got near he heard neighing and realised it was a pegasus stable. A pegasus wouldn't be able to fly high enough to reach the *Hybris*, he thought, dismissing the building and running to the next one. On his third try, he gave a shout of triumph. Tethered to short posts inside a squat marble hut were two rows of longboats.

Movement caught his eye in the back of the dark building and he stilled, wishing he could see better. A flash of red made him step forward.

'Lyssa?' he called. A figure moved towards him, taking form as she neared the light.

'Hercules,' his daughter answered. She really had inherited his fierceness, he thought, savouring the hatred leaking from her.

'How's that big slave of yours?'

'Epizon is fine,' she spat. 'He's not my slave. And I'll make sure you pay a hundred times over for what you could have done to him.'

'I doubt that,' he said, folding his arms across his chest. He did not want a fist fight with the girl. Not now. Every moment he was talking to her, Theseus and the giants were getting ahead of him. Lyssa had clearly had the same thought, as she took a step backwards, her fists flexing at her sides.

'Just wait, Hercules. I need to win this Trial, for a friend who's more important than you, but next time, I will kill you.' Venom dripped from the tiny girl's voice and a shiver of excitement rippled through Hercules.

'I'm looking forward to it, *daughter*.'

Rage flooded the girl's face and she reached down and tore a longboat from its tether. He ducked as she roared and launched the boat at him. It flew harmlessly over his head.

'You have more strength than I thought,' he said, chuckling as he straightened up. 'But you're no match for me.'

'Go to hell, Hercules,' she hissed, and disappeared into the dark again. A second later a longboat shot from the back of the building, sailing over him and out into the sky.

He would enjoy killing her, he thought, as he untied the nearest boat and climbed in. He really would.

16

'I'm telling you, Captain, we have the perfect tool for this!' insisted Busiris as they came to a stop behind the stable.

'No,' growled Antaeus, cracking his knuckles. 'We go after Diomedes.'

'That won't help us capture a mare! We need the net you made on Scorpio.' Busiris was doing a poor job keeping the frustration from his voice.

'We fight Diomedes,' huffed Albion, and Bergion grunted in agreement with his brother.

'One giant can't beat three,' he said.

'Exactly,' agreed Antaeus.

'But, Captain, the mares are still dangerous,' Busiris tried again, calmly this time. 'We need a way to get close to them without being burned by their flames.'

Although he was reluctant to admit it, Eryx agreed with Busiris. They'd gone to great lengths to make that chain net, and it was exactly what they needed.

'Maybe two of us should go back to the *Orion* and get it,'

he said quietly. Antaeus glared at him. 'Captain, nobody else has anything like it. It might be what tips the balance.'

Antaeus pushed his hand through his dark hair, his face screwing up in thought. 'Fine,' he said eventually.' Busiris, you go. But just you.'

'But, Captain—' Busiris started to splutter.

'I'm not losing any fighters! If you want to go, go now. There will be longboats at the palace.' Antaeus pointed to where they could just see the huge building, framed in the dim light. Busiris looked from Antaeus's face to his pointing hand, then closed his mouth. With a final scowl he turned and began to jog into the darkness.

'Will he be able to lift the net?' Eryx asked hesitantly.

'Of course he will. He may be small but he's still half giant,' his captain snapped.

Eryx said nothing, but thought about when he'd carried the net through Hephaestus's forge. There was no way he would have been able to carry it without Antaeus.

17

HEDONE

Hedone didn't want to be digging a hole in the dark. She didn't want to be avoiding Psyche's disappointed glares. She wanted to be with Hercules, walking on the beach, watching the glistening water, sharing her hopes and dreams while her fingers entwined with his.

'How much more?' she asked, her voice strained.

Theseus straightened up and looked at her. He'd broken off large branches for them to dig with, and he and Psyche had made much more progress than she had.

'Quite a bit,' he said from the middle of the hole they'd made. It barely reached his knees. 'The horses are a lot bigger than I am.' He smiled. She groaned, and dug her stick into the ground angrily.

'Concentrate on making it wider, not deeper,' said Psyche. 'It's easier on your back.'

'What do you care about my back?' she grumbled. Psyche sighed and said nothing, digging her own much larger branch into the earth.

. . .

THEY DUG for what seemed like an eternity to Hedone. Psyche had been right about her back. Just a small amount of bending began sending aches through her muscles, and she found sticking to the shallower edge and widening the pit was easier.

'I do care, you know,' said Psyche quietly, from behind her. Hedone glanced at her.

'Then you would be happy for me. This is what I've wanted my whole life.'

'I thought you wanted... someone else.' Psyche shot a pointed look at Theseus, who was still digging, not looking at either of them.

A flash of memory pulled at her gut, the uneasy feeling that had been coming less and less often clawing at the edges of her mind.

'No,' she said firmly. 'I wanted love. Real, true love.'

'We all want that, Hedone. But love makes us blind.'

'You don't know him. You know what others say about him, what the gods want us to think. If Zeus loves him, that should be testament enough!' She stood up straight, turning to Psyche. Theseus stopped, and leaned on his branch.

'Zeus has his own agenda, Hedone,' he said.

She glared at him. 'So you're on her side?'

'It's not about sides—' Theseus started, but Psyche cut him off.

'Yes, Captain, it is. *Hercules* is not on our side. If she's with him, then she's not with us.'

Pain twisted in Hedone's stomach at her words. They were going to throw her off the crew. Wasn't that what she wanted? She wanted to be with Hercules, on the *Hybris*. She *needed* to be with him. Then why did she feel so betrayed, so panicked?

'She doesn't need to choose yet,' said Theseus gently.

'Stop talking about me like I'm not here,' Hedone snapped, hot tears stinging her eyes again. 'You always treat me like a child. I'm sick of it!'

'Shhhh!' said Theseus, across her. She whirled around, about to shout at him for proving her point, when she saw the frown on his face as he peered out of the now shoulder-deep pit. Two male voices were just discernible in the distance, and she fell silent, listening.

'Ab, I'm serious, you can't do this.'

'Yes, I can. I bet it's not occurred to anybody to just ask him.'

'For good reason! Did you see him?'

'We don't want to hurt the horses, just capture one, temporarily. I'm sure Diomedes won't have a problem with that.'

'You're as mad as those creatures! He's not going to let you do this, Ab. Just wait for Lyssa to come back.'

'And lose the chance to get my legs back? No way, Phyleus. I'm doing this.'

'I'm sorry, truly, but I can't let you go over there.'

'I'd like to see you stop me.'

There was a shout, then, 'Nestor, stop him!'

THESEUS PUT his hands on the edge of the pit and hauled himself up quickly. Hedone and Psyche scrambled to follow him.

18

EVADNE

Evadne stepped forward involuntarily as she saw the boy in the wheelchair racing towards the stable. What was he doing? He had been cocky, she remembered, in the cage on Capricorn, but she hadn't had him down as a fighter. Lyssa wouldn't use him as bait, surely? The fierce centaur who had joined Lyssa's crew was charging after him, and the other man, Phyleus, was behind them both. She frowned, then her mouth fell open as Abderos shouted, 'Diomedes!'

The boy rolled to a stop by the stable, out of range of the snickering mares. The centaur skidded to a halt behind him, clearly wary of the beasts.

Diomedes' booming footsteps shook the ground and Evadne edged forward. The giant appeared again, too distant for her to make out the features above his long, snarled beard. As he emerged from the stable he looked around, growing in height every second.

'Who calls me?' he rumbled.

'Me, Abderos,' the boy shouted. Diomedes spotted him and paused.

'You are sitting down?'

'Er, yeah. Look, I wondered if we could borrow one of your horses. Just for a few minutes?'

Evadne couldn't believe her ears. He was asking for one of the horses? Was he completely mad?

Diomedes stared at Abderos for a long moment, then began laughing, a massive, deep, echoing laugh that went on and on. Spotting movement to her right, Evadne saw Theseus drawing up on the other side of the horses, panting slightly.

'You, small sitting boy, have the nerve to ask me for one of my horses?' Diomedes gasped through laughs. He was still growing, now almost as tall as the stable building.

'Only for a few minutes,' said Abderos. Gods, but the kid had nerve, thought Evadne. A thought struck her. Or enough motivation... Aphrodite's wish. She remembered the story he had told them in the cage, about losing his legs in the fighting pits. An emotion she didn't recognise rose in her chest, pity mingled with respect and sadness and... hope. She wanted Diomedes to say yes, she realised. Let this boy win with no bloodshed. Let him wish for his legs.

'Nobody has ever asked Diomedes for such a thing before,' the giant said, his laughs beginning to subside. A speck on the horizon was growing behind the stable and Evadne squinted at it. It was a longboat.

'Perhaps... Perhaps the boy's courage should be rewarded,' Diomedes mused, tilting his massive head to one side. The longboat had almost reached the stable and Evadne could see a glowing red light above it. *Keravnos*.

THE BOAT SWOOPED low over Abderos as it reached them, and Hercules leaned over the edge, swiping his lethal blade at Diomedes' neck. A crimson line bubbled up where the blade had cut, and the giant roared, swiping at the boat as he stumbled. Hercules manoeuvred it lower, leaping to the ground as Diomedes crashed to his knees, grabbing at the stables for support. The wood croaked and moaned, then collapsed under his weight, blood seeping into the earth as his head followed his massive body and hit the ground.

EVADNE DIDN'T KNOW if it was the scent of so much blood or the death of their master, but the horses went wild. They screeched and whinnied, pulling at the chains tethering them to the brazier and rearing up on their back legs. Streams of fire burst from them every few seconds, illuminating the grisly scene.

She could see Hercules clearly as he turned to Abderos, who was sitting stock still in his chair. As Hercules stalked towards him, Evadne moved forward, throwing her hands out in vain.

'No!' she cried. Bile rose in her throat as Hercules lifted the boy from his chair and threw him at the raging horses' stamping feet.

19

LYSSA

Time seemed to stand still as Lyssa's longboat crested the stables and she saw Hercules throwing Abderos to the mares. She couldn't hear his cries as the flames shot from their jaws, their hooves trampled his prostrate body, their teeth tore into his flesh. It was like someone else was watching.

'Lyssa!' Phyleus's voice broke through the numb horror. 'Lyssa, he's...'

Phyleus knew. Phyleus knew when somebody was about to die.

'No...' she whispered.

'It's too late,' he choked.

She aimed the boat down, straight towards Hercules.

RAGE FLOODED HER BODY, so strong it felt like she would explode. Her limbs felt bigger, her body felt faster, her mind and muscles strained to hold in the power. Red seeped into the edges of her vision and she couldn't hear anything but a distant rushing.

Before the boat reached the ground she leaped from it, landing hard on Hercules's back. He roared, trying to flip her over his shoulder, but she reached around his neck, pulling at the arm that held *Keravnos*. He resisted her and she pulled harder, willing more strength into her body. She swore she felt a distant snap, something painful and liberating at the same time. The red in her vision turned black. She could feel every nerve in her body, every movement of Hercules beneath her. And she knew she was stronger than him. She *hated* more than him. She *cared* more than him. She would make him pay for every hurt he had caused.

With a scream, she gripped his cloak with one hand, leaned back and smashed her other fist into the side of his head. He stumbled sideways, and she reached over his shoulder and twisted his arm again. *Keravnos* hit the ground with a thud and she dropped from Hercules's back, rolling towards the sword. He lunged for it but she was faster, picking it up as she rolled to her feet and swinging it towards him. For a split second the glowing sword fell lifeless, and weighed more than she could bear, then it suddenly hummed with power, shining bright and red, feeling like an extension of her own body. She barely registered the flash of fear on Hercules's face as she whirled the sword towards the mares, still screaming. They reared and jumped, avoiding both the blade and the girl with power pouring from her body as she tore towards them.

'Leave him alone!' she screamed as she hacked as hard as she could at the nearest horse, only to miss it and hit the huge brazier instead. It creaked, then started to topple, and she whirled around again, slashing at anything within reach. She was stronger than him. *Him*. Where was he? She turned back, holding the sword in both hands, trying to see clearly through the haze. Where was he?

A mare had broken free of the fallen brazier and was galloping past him, fire bursting from its mouth. Hercules threw himself at it, grabbing at its back.

No! He couldn't win! Not after what he had done! *He would die for what he had done*. She ran forward, the power in her legs moving her faster than she'd ever run before, and she closed the gap between them in seconds. His lunge for the mare had missed and he backed away as she advanced.

'You sick, twisted, miserable piece of shit,' she hissed, raising the sword high above her head. Hercules took another step back, pulling his cloak across himself, his face hard. She would make sure he never took another breath, if it was the last thing she did. Power coursed through her, flowed into the sword, spilled out of her skin. She would take his life, right now. His and anyone else who didn't deserve to live.

'We have a victor.' Aphrodite's sweet voice rang through the air.

The second Lyssa looked away, Hercules kicked at her hand, and *Keravnos* tumbled from her grip. Convulsions seized her muscles instantly, as they did when her connection to the *Alastor* was broken. She crumpled to the ground, gasping for breath, the pain in her ribs and shoulder intensifying with the crippling seizures.

'You can't handle the power yet,' Hercules said softly from above her. 'But I know that look. I know that power. We are the same, daughter,' he whispered. 'It's a shame we never got better acquainted after all.'

Lyssa didn't have the strength to look up at him. Her chest was convulsing so hard she couldn't get enough air. But she knew he was raising the sword for the final blow.

She had failed. Failed Abderos, Epizon, the whole of Olympus.

'I SAID, WE HAVE A VICTOR!' Aphrodite's voice blasted across them, and Lyssa's aching body froze, as though time had stopped. The convulsions still wracked her insides but she couldn't move a muscle. Slowly, her body rose from the ground, her frame tipping until she was righted. She moved her eyes, trying to look around, and saw Hercules, sword raised, floating along beside her. They drifted towards the collapsed stable, where Diomedes' body was still leaking blood into the ground.

'Lyssa! Oh, thank the gods, Lyssa.' Phyleus's voice was frantic in her head. With a pulse of pain, her frozen body came back to life, and she dropped to her hands and knees, gasping. Phyleus and Len rushed to her side, both speaking too fast for her to make sense of their words.

'HEROES, IF YOU PLEASE,' Aphrodite said.

They all fell silent and Lyssa raised her head. The goddess was standing next to the fallen brazier. And at her feet lay Abderos. Abderos's mangled body.

A heaving sob threatened to choke Lyssa, and acid burned her throat. She tried to turn away too late, emptying her stomach on the ground in front of her. Burning tears scorched her face as she heaved again and again. How had she failed him so miserably? He was sixteen years old. And now... She looked up weakly, what was left of his blood-streaked face blurring through her tears.

'Abderos,' she moaned aloud, falling back onto her heels and covering her face with her hands. 'Ab, I'm so sorry.'

20

EVADNE

E vadne couldn't look at Lyssa. She couldn't look at the boy's broken, torn body. Hercules had tossed him to those creatures like a snack. Her stomach turned again and she closed her eyes. It didn't stop her from hearing Lyssa's heaving sobs. Would Hercules cry like that for her? Of course he wouldn't.

ON SAGITTARIUS, she had aimed a crossbow at Lyssa. She had been prepared to pull the trigger. To kill another being. How? How could she possibly have thought she was capable of that? Why would anyone want to live forever, with murder on their conscience? Her roiling stomach churned even harder when she thought about sharing her bed with Hercules. He had touched her, kissed her body, been *inside* her. She rubbed at her crawling skin. He was a monster. No prize was worth this. No fortune or fame could justify Lyssa's awful grief. She opened her eyes and found herself looking for Eryx. He was standing ten feet away, face pale. His words rang in her mind. *You're on your own, Evadne.*

. . .

Aphrodite coughed and everyone's attention snapped to her.

'Are you done?' the goddess asked Lyssa, rolling her eyes.

Lyssa glared back at Aphrodite, gulping back sobs. Phyleus crouched beside her and the little satyr stood protectively in front of her, tears rolling down both their faces. The centaur stood close behind them, her expression so fierce that Evadne almost stepped backwards. A deep longing bubbled up inside her, overwhelming her practised emotions. They had no fame or fortune, and they didn't need it. They were a family.

'As many of you were too...' Aphrodite fished for the right word and Evadne looked back at the beautiful goddess. '... *busy* to see what happened, I'll enlighten you.' She smiled. 'When Lyssa broke the brazier and inadvertently freed the mares, the clever, clever Theseus saw a chance to lure one over to the trap he had dug. It fell in and was immediately incapacitated.' She beamed at Theseus. He didn't smile back.

'You may have a day to choose your wish,' she said, her voice like honey.

'I don't need a day, divine Aphrodite,' Theseus said, bowing his head.

Aphrodite raised her perfect eyebrows.

'Oh, really? Then wish away, my hero.'

'I was trapped in the cage with Abderos on Capricorn. He was courageous, and good. I wish for you to bring him back.'

Behind him, Lyssa scrabbled to her feet, her tear-streaked face alight with hope.

'Is this Abderos?' Aphrodite looked down at the boy's body. Theseus nodded. 'That's what you would do with a wish from the gods? Not wealth, or strength, or love?' the goddess cooed.

Theseus shook his head.

'He didn't deserve to die.'

'Many who die don't deserve to,' Aphrodite answered quietly. Theseus stared into her beautiful face. 'Fine,' she said eventually. 'I'll need to... arrange it with Hades, but I can't see why not. He will be restored just as he was, though, before you get any ideas.'

Theseus nodded.

'Thank you, divine goddess. You are as kind as you are beautiful.'

A slow smile spread across her face.

'Yes. Of course. Now, your next Trial will be announced at midday tomorrow. Rest well, heroes.' She vanished in a flash of white light, along with Abderos's body.

Evadne stared at the spot. How could people like Theseus exist alongside brutes like Hercules? And how had she been so close to becoming one of Hercules's kind?

ARES

THE IMMORTALITY TRIALS

TRIAL NINE

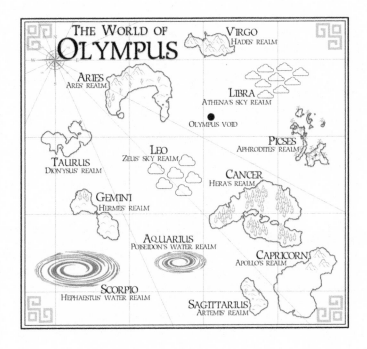

1

LYSSA

A bright flash of light pierced Lyssa's eyelids and she lifted her head from her arms. She must have fallen asleep sitting at the galley table, she thought groggily.

'Captain?' a small voice said, and she turned her head quickly.

'Abderos,' she breathed, and launched herself from her seat towards him. He was there, in their galley, in his chair, whole and well. 'Gods Ab, I'm so, so sorry,' she sobbed as she threw her arms around him.

'I- I- What happened?' he muttered through her hair. 'I remember talking to Diomedes... then...'

Lyssa felt him stiffen.

'I died...' he whispered.

'Theseus restored you,' she told him, taking a deep breath and sitting back on her heels to look at him. He seemed perfect.

'Cap, you're crying.' Abderos frowned.

'Yeah. Yeah, that's happened quite a bit lately.' She

smiled, wiping at the tears with the back of her wrist. 'Ab, I thought we'd lost you.'

'Theseus brought me back? How?'

'With Aphrodite's wish. He won the Trial.'

'I... I wanted that wish,' Abderos said, quietly, looking down at his lap. Lyssa's heart ached for him and she gripped his arms hard.

'We'll find another way, Ab. What matters now is that you're here. With us. Alive!'

He smiled at her.

'Alive. Of course. That is definitely more important. Why would Theseus use his wish on me?'

'He said he met you in the cage on Capricorn and that you were too brave to die.'

'Really? He said that?' A proud smile spread across Abderos's face. 'Maybe he'll let me see his Typhoon, if he likes me that much.'

Overwhelming relief washed over Lyssa and she laughed aloud as new tears spilled down her cheeks.

'Only you, Ab. Only you can come back from the dead and be this calm about it!'

'I don't remember it.' He shrugged. 'I just know somehow that I wasn't here any more.'

Lyssa sent a silent prayer of thanks to Aphrodite and Hades, for whichever of them had made sure he didn't remember the horses.

'Come on, the rest of the crew will want to see you,' she said, getting to her feet.

'Aye, aye, Cap,' he said, and rolled his chair after her.

Everyone was asleep, but Lyssa projected the news to them anyway. They would all want to know that Ab was back.

Len and Phyleus were on deck in under two minutes, Epizon limping up moments later alongside Nestor. Lyssa didn't try to hide her silent tears of relief as she leaned against the railings. There was no point pretending she was strong enough to contain her emotions. Not any more. Abderos was back, and nothing else mattered. She drank in the sight of him, laughing with Phyleus and Len as they clinked glasses of ouzo.

'I'M sorry I wasn't there, Lyssa,' Epizon said, leaning against the railings next to her. 'Watching in the flame dish was the hardest thing I've ever had to do in my life.'

'It's not your fault, Epizon. It was mine.'

'No, it wasn't. Diomedes was going to give Abderos the mare, you know.' Lyssa looked at Epizon. 'Hercules is the only person to blame.' His face hardened as he spoke.

'Epizon... He said something to me.'

'You nearly killed him, Lyssa. I've never seen you so strong or fast.'

'It was that sword. It's like... It's like being connected to the *Alastor*, but instead of infinite freedom I felt infinite strength. I... I wanted to kill.'

'You nearly had him, you were so close. You'll get another chance.'

'No, Ep, that's not what I mean. I mean, I wanted to kill him *and* everyone else who deserved it. And Hercules saw it. He told me I was like him.' Her skin crawled at the memory.

'You're nothing like him.' Epizon shook his head. 'That must have just been the power of the sword.'

Lyssa looked away doubtfully. She had felt the fringes of that power before. The invincibility, the belief that she was stronger, faster, more divine than everyone else. The knowledge that she could take whatever she liked. *Keravnos* hadn't been the source of that power. It had just amplified it.

'Where do you think we're going next?' Epizon asked her.

'I don't know,' she answered with a small shrug. Tiredness was seeping into her, now that Abderos was back and her anxiety was lessening. 'They say they're picking the realms at random but we've not had any of the big three gods yet. Bit of a coincidence.'

'We can't go to Virgo,' Epizon said abruptly. She looked at him.

'We're going to have to go, if the Trial is there. I thought you always wanted to see Virgo?'

'I... I did. I can't explain it.' He frowned, looking around vaguely. 'Whenever I think about Virgo I feel like something truly awful is about to happen. Like there's nothing more important than not going. I don't know why.'

'Right,' said Lyssa slowly. 'Well... I guess we'll deal with that when we have to.'

He gave her an uneasy look.

2

HEDONE

'Hedone, please come up on deck. We need to talk.' Theseus's voice rang in her head and Hedone dragged the pillow away from her face with a groan. She didn't want to talk to the others. She already knew what they would say. She had slept badly after they had been spirited back to the *Virtus*. Theseus had won another Trial, and Hercules wouldn't be happy about it. Worse, they were saying Hercules was the one who had killed the boy Theseus had wished back to life. How was it that her object of her love was so misunderstood? She rolled out of bed, rubbing her bleary eyes. When they were married and this was all over, they would all see. They would see what she saw. The soft, tender, proud man.

'I'll be up shortly,' she thought back to Theseus, and sighed as she entered her washroom to get ready.

SHE STEPPED HESITANTLY OUT of the hauler and onto the quarterdeck. The sky was a bright, bright blue, as it often was over Pisces. White clouds sparkled around them and she took a long breath. Theseus stood up from the captain's chair when he saw her.

'Morning, Captain,' she said.

'Morning, Hedone,' he answered. She strolled as casually as she could to the railings, and looked out over the island, surrounded by glittering turquoise ocean.

'Where do you think we're going next?' she asked.

'It doesn't matter where we're going next.' Psyche's voice was hard and blunt behind her. Hedone turned around slowly.

'Psyche, I know we're not going to agree on this, but it doesn't mean we can't still be friends,' she said.

'Hedone, open your eyes, girl! He threw an unarmed boy to his death!'

'You're wrong!' Hedone yelled back at her, her temper flaring as she stamped her foot on the deck. 'You didn't see him do it, they're lying!'

'The whole of Olympus saw him do it; they can't all be lying! What is the matter with you?' The woman threw her hands in the air as she spoke, her dark braids swinging. She was a fool, Hedone thought. A fool who believed Hera's lies. Hercules couldn't have done such a thing.

'There is nothing the matter with me,' she spat. 'You are the one who is jaded. Hera will go to any length to ruin the life of her husband's illegitimate son.'

'Hedone, *I* saw him do it.' Theseus spoke quietly. She turned to him, seeing sadness on his handsome, open face.

'No,' she said, shaking her head. 'You saw wrong.'

'I reached the stables before you both. Hercules lifted Abderos from his chair and threw him to the horses. Hedone, we can't make your decisions for you, but you must know that he is dangerous.'

Doubt, clear and cold, seeped into Hedone. Theseus

wasn't a liar. She knew that. But why would Hercules do such a thing? What would possess him to kill someone who posed no threat?

'Why?' she whispered, hot tears burning at the back of her eyes.

'It distracted the horses.'

She shook her head.

'There's something we don't know. There must be. He wouldn't...' she faltered. The uneasy feeling was growing, twisting in her gut. She stared at Theseus, his brown eyes, his square jaw, his soft skin. There was something she didn't know. Something wrong. She groped and pulled at her memory, grasping at the hidden thread. And suddenly, she caught it. It was Theseus she used to love. Anger washed over her as she looked at her captain. How had she ever wanted him? He was manipulative, cunning and cruel. She had spent years trying to seduce him and he had continually spurned her, never giving her what she desired. Why was she on his crew? Why did she still stand beside him?

'Why have you never wanted me?' she blurted, tears spilling from her eyes.

Theseus flinched, looking away.

'Hedone, you're beyond beautiful. Of course I've wanted you. But...' he trailed off and Psyche stamped her booted foot.

'Captain, just tell her,' she snapped.

'My heart belongs to another. It has for a very long time.'

Hedone's mouth fell open.

'But... But you share your bed with women all the time! With Aphrodite, even.'

'I can't say no to a goddess,' he said. 'And the other women mean nothing. You... You would not mean nothing.'

'Why did you keep me close? Why did you let me make

a fool of myself?' Her face felt like it was on fire, shame and anger making her head pound. All this time she had never had a chance? All this time she could have been with Hercules?

'You were so impressionable when you left the temple, I couldn't let you fall into the wrong hands.'

'I'm not a damn toy!' she shouted, surprising herself with the venom in her voice. 'You've used me! Kept me away from anyone who might actually love me back!'

'Hedone, if that's true then I'm sorry, I truly am, but Hercules isn't—'

'I'm not talking about this any more!' She choked on a sob as she whirled around, heading for the hauler as quickly as she could. She needed to be away from him. She needed to find a way off the ship.

3

LYSSA

'Captain! Captain, Captain, Captain!' The urgent words dragged Lyssa from sleep.

'What?'

'Captain, you need to get up on deck, now.' Abderos's voice rang in her mind. She sat bolt upright.

'What's wrong? Are you OK?'

'We have a visitor. An important visitor.' His mental voice thrummed with excitement.

'Who?' she answered, kicking her sheets off.

'Athena,' he whispered.

'Shit,' she said, and scrabbled out of her bunk.

She grabbed some worn trousers from the floor, pulled them on, and darted from her chambers, still wearing the shirt she had slept in. She didn't spare a thought for her bare feet or un-brushed hair as she skidded into the hauler. *Athena?* What did she want? Please, please, gods let her be here to help them. Maybe she would give her a magic sword like Hercules's.

. . .

'Captain Lyssa.' The goddess's beautiful voice calmed her hammering heart as soon as she stepped onto the deck. Athena was standing under the shimmering sails by the main mast, regal and stunning.

'Athena,' Lyssa said, and bowed low. She scanned the deck quickly but could only see Abderos up on the quarterdeck.

'I'm sorry to cut your rest short. But I need to speak with you on an urgent matter.'

'Of course, Athena,' she answered.

'I am about to tell you something that I am forbidden to discuss, so it is very important that you do not share it.'

'May my crew know?'

Athena assessed her for a moment.

'Yes,' she said eventually, and flicked her wrist. With a small flash, the rest of the crew appeared on the deck, accompanied by cries of surprise and confusion. Nestor clicked her hooves on the deck as she looked around and Epizon, to the centaur's right, was wide-eyed and alert. He was shirtless and Lyssa gaped at the wound in his shoulder until she heard a spluttered protest behind her.

'What the...?' She turned and gasped. Phyleus was standing behind her and he was completely naked. He had his hands together over his crotch and his face was aflame under his damp hair.

'I was bathing,' he said through gritted teeth. Lyssa's eyes raked involuntarily over his body, beads of water still rolling down his bare chest. Power hummed to life under her skin and her core tensed.

'Apologies, human,' Athena said, and suddenly a large cloak covered Phyleus from head to foot. He fumbled around beneath it and Lyssa choked back a laugh as his head popped out of the thick material. He glared at her.

'Athena needs to talk to us,' Lyssa said loudly to the crew. Everyone bowed to the goddess and she inclined her head.

'During the Trials there has been an... incident in the world of the gods. Hades has broken a very sacred rule. And Zeus has punished him cruelly. The gods have few limitations but we are not creatures of prophecy and none of us know what the implications of Hades' actions may be.' She looked at all of them in turn, her gaze lingering on Epizon.

'Hades has lost something and we would all like to find it.'

Lyssa stared at the goddess. What was she asking?

'Athena, I don't know how we can help you. We are bound to the Trials.'

'It is my belief that you have already come across that which we seek.'

Lyssa screwed up her face.

'What is it?'

'Ah, but that is the wrong question.' Athena smiled. 'Not what, but who.'

Tenebrae. The second Lyssa thought the name, pain lanced through her skull. She heard shouts from around her as she squeezed her eyes closed, then suddenly, the pain stopped. Athena stepped towards her as she opened her eyes.

'Where is she?' the goddess asked gently.

Lyssa opened her mouth to speak, but nothing came out. She frowned, moving her lips, trying in vain to make a sound. Athena's eyes narrowed and she turned to Epizon, whose dark skin was pale. His eyes were wide and fearful and he shook his head noiselessly.

'She has power,' murmured Athena. 'She must be on this ship.' Athena looked to Lyssa for confirmation but Lyssa couldn't move her head to nod. Athena put her hand to her mouth thoughtfully.

'Keep her here. Keep her secret and safe,' she said, then vanished in a flash of blinding white light.

'What just happened?' stammered Phyleus. Lyssa worked her jaw, testing her voice nervously. To her relief, she could speak again.

'Did Tenebrae do that? Stop us talking?'

'She shouldn't be able to, she's not been out in the light since Lady Lamia,' said Len.

Lyssa turned to Epizon.

'What do you...' She trailed off as she looked at him. His eyes were unfocused and his skin was still pale. 'Epizon?' She stepped towards him, laying her hand on his arm. He jumped and frowned at her.

'Athena said to keep her safe,' he said.

'I know, but... She just stopped the entire crew from speaking. We didn't know she could do that.'

'What else can she do?' Phyleus asked quietly. Epizon looked sharply at him.

'It doesn't matter. Athena told us to keep her safe.'

'Yeah, but didn't that freak you out?'

'Just keep her safe!' Epizon shouted, pulling his arm from Lyssa's hand and marching towards the hauler.

'Ep, wait,' called Lyssa, but he ignored her, yanking open the hauler door and stepping in. 'Len, what's wrong with him?' She frowned, turning to the satyr. 'He's acting really strange about going to Virgo, which is Hades' realm. He's been sitting down there with the tank every spare minute since she told him her name. Is she... doing something to him?'

Len looked up at her uneasily.

'He was unconscious on the cargo deck with her for two

days. I guess it's possible she got into his head somehow. But I still don't think there's enough light down there for her to be dangerous.'

'Len, she has enough power to stop us talking to a god.' Lyssa put her hands on her hips as she spoke.

'Yeah. I guess she does. I wonder what she's got to do with Hades?'

Lyssa glanced at Phyleus. He caught her looking and pulled the massive cloak tighter around himself.

'Don't ask me, I just got Hades' residual powers. I have no more idea about this than you do,' he told her mentally. She sighed. She would talk to Epizon after the Trial announcement, when he would hopefully be more himself.

'You look ridiculous, by the way,' she said silently to Phyleus.

'Have you seen your hair?' he shot back.

She scowled at him.

'I'm going back to the bath,' Phyleus said out loud.

'Good idea,' she gave him a sarcastic smile.

'Wanna join me?' he added silently. She flushed and barely stopped herself sending back the word 'Yes.'

Eryx roared as he launched himself at Bergion. The giant was too slow to side-step him, and Eryx's fist slammed into his ribs as they stumbled backwards together.

'Ow!' yelled Bergion.

Eryx bounced backwards, panting.

'Sorry,' he said.

'You said you wanted to train, not fight,' growled the giant, rubbing at his side. 'I wasn't ready. This is no fun. I'm going for a drink.' Bergion's footsteps echoed around the massive cargo deck as he ambled off to the hauler.

Eryx sighed. He'd have to burn off some of his anger alone. He bounced on the balls of his feet, dropping his shoulders and raising his fists in a fighting stance.

'One, two,' he counted aloud, throwing punches into the empty air in front of him.

Nobody listened to him. Why did nobody listen to him? *One, two.* He had told Antaeus that Busiris couldn't manage the net alone.

At least Theseus had won, instead of Hercules.

Abderos's broken body flashed in his mind. *One, two.* Theseus was a good man. It wouldn't be so bad if he won instead of them. Eryx wasn't even sure if he wanted to be immortal any more. After all, what was the point of him living forever if nobody else cared what he thought? *One, two.* Sweat dripped into his eyes but he ignored it. What if Evadne cared what he thought? Would he want to be immortal then? *One, two.* He punched out too hard, feeling his shoulder muscle pulling painfully. He'd meant what he said to her. Even before he'd seen Hercules kill a defenceless man. He'd rather be a nobody than live with that.

'Eryx, it's nearly midday. Come to the flame dish.' Antaeus's voice sounded in his head.

'Yes, Captain.' He dragged his arm across his forehead, wiping away sweat. He didn't feel any better.

THE FLAMES LEAPED to life as Eryx topped the stairs to the quarterdeck and the blond announcer smiled from the dish.

'Good day, Olympus! What can I say but *wow*! It's been a rough ride so far for some of the heroes! I bet you can't wait to see what's in store for them next...' He faded with a wink, then the hulking, gleaming figure of Ares solidified in the flames. Albion and Bergion gave a small cheer and Busiris beamed. The realm of war was their home.

'Heroes,' the god boomed. 'You will be set your challenge by a queen of my realm. Journey to Aries, and I will speak with you in one hour.' He vanished.

'A queen? Which one do you think it is?' asked Eryx. They all looked at Busiris.

'There are many queens on Aries.' He shrugged, but he was still smiling. 'And most will look favourably on a king of Aries like me.'

Hercules stared into the flames long after Ares had disappeared. He had underestimated his daughter, loath as he was to admit it. The look in her eyes when she held *Keravnos* had been unmistakable. She bore the same killing urge, the same torrent of power he did. He *must* kill her. And soon.

'Evadne, get me some wine,' he projected at the girl.

'Yes, Captain,' came her response.

He sighed as he sat back in his plush chair. He was fed up of these games now. Of being toyed with by the gods. Each of the crews had two wins, despite him being stronger, faster and more gifted than any of the others. How had that happened? The giants were strong, but they also had that clever king of Egypt on their crew. Theseus had the fierce fighting woman, Psyche, permanently at his side. Lyssa... Lyssa had gotten lucky. Sure, she could make her ship move fast, but her win on Taurus was down to having that prince on her crew. All of the captains had so much help, Hercules thought, running his fingers across his stubbled jaw. Zeus had told him to use Evadne but that wasn't working. Did he still need her?

On cue, she appeared at the top of the quarterdeck steps, holding a glass of wine. She held it out to him without a word.

'Do you know what the tonic we won on Scorpio does yet?' he asked her.

'No, Captain.' She shook her head and turned to go.

'Are you frightened of me, Evadne?'

The girl turned around slowly.

'Sometimes, Captain,' she answered, avoiding his gaze.

Hercules thought about that.

'Good,' he said eventually. 'Go and read. Find out what that tonic does.' He waved his hand at her.

'Yes, Captain,' she said, and hurried down the stairs.

What a difference a short time had made to her, he thought. She had been so full of fight, and attitude. He had broken her well and fully, as he'd known he would.

His thoughts drifted to Hedone. She did not need breaking. She needed nothing but his love, his care, his touch. Next time he saw her, they would devise a plan for her to join the *Hybris*. He could not be without her much longer.

6

LYSSA

'Ah. I see you brushed your hair.' Phyleus grinned at Lyssa as he stepped out of the hauler onto the quarterdeck.

'And I see you found some clothes.' She smiled back from her captain's chair.

'I could lose them again, if you like.' He raised his eyebrows at her, eyes sparkling. Lyssa forced herself to hold his gaze, willing heat not to rise to her cheeks. She could play this game.

'I've seen better, to be honest,' she said, with a tilt of her head.

'You obviously weren't looking hard enough. Here, try again.' He stepped towards her and began pulling his shirt up his chest.

'Whoa,' Lyssa said, waving her hands, eyes fixed on his bare stomach. 'That won't be necessary.'

'It's not supposed to be necessary. It's supposed to be fun.' He let go of his shirt but took another step towards her. 'Ab's alive and well, Epizon is on the mend and we have time until the next Trial. It's the perfect time for fun.'

'Phyleus, I don't think I'm in a position to be thinking about fun. We're on our way to the realm of war. Doesn't exactly scream fun.'

He sighed.

'Gotta take fun where you can get it.'

'Is that one of your lines? I bet a few young ladies have fallen for that haughty charm of yours.'

'You think I'm charming?' His mouth quirked into a smile and Lyssa rolled her eyes. But she did think he was charming. More than charming. How had that faint physical attraction she'd felt when he first joined the crew turned into the overwhelming desire she felt now? Every time she had needed somebody during these Trials, he had been there. He'd pushed her from the longboat mast when her powers might have overcome her on Sagittarius. He'd dived into the ocean and pulled her from the water on Scorpio. He'd given his own blood to save her best friend. He'd held her when she thought she'd lost Abderos. He'd kissed her when she'd needed to escape. Why was she fighting him?

'Yes,' she said. His eyebrows flew up in surprise and she laughed. 'What are you going to do if I start being nice to you? You won't know what to say to me.'

'Lyssa, all I want is for you to be nice to me,' he said quietly. 'And I don't mean, you know, physically. I mean I want us to... to...' His cheeks were turning pink and Lyssa's heart pounded in her chest.

'I know what you mean,' she told him. 'It's not something I've ever thought about before, though. Sharing myself, my life with someone.' She looked away as she spoke and he crouched down in front of her, taking her hand.

'You already do that, with your crew,' he said.

'That's not the same.' She met his eyes.

'Well, given the things I want to do to you, I hope not,' he said, and a thrill shuddered through her at the look in his eyes. 'But seriously, you don't need to do anything differently. I've never met anybody like you. You're so incredibly strong.'

Lyssa gave a small, involuntary laugh.

'Granddaughter of the lord of the gods.' She smiled.

'I don't mean strong like that! Although that is quite sexy. I mean, I've had spoiled princesses and pretentious academics pushed at me since I was sixteen years old and you... You're fierce and bold and real.' He squeezed her hand hard and fixed his eyes on hers.

'You're my captain.'

In that one sentence, Lyssa made her decision. Phyleus didn't want to change her, to challenge her, to conquer her. He just wanted to be with her. She leaned forward, slowly, and felt his hand tense around hers as she brought her lips to his.

'Say that again,' she murmured as she closed her eyes.

'You're my captain,' he breathed, and kissed her.

'Sorry to interrupt, Captain.' Lyssa leaped back from Phyleus, her back slamming into her chair, and he stood up quickly. She turned, seeing Epizon smiling as he walked stiffly across the quarterdeck towards them. 'It's been just about an hour, we should hear from Ares soon.'

'Right, course, yeah,' Lyssa stammered, getting quickly out of the chair. 'Sit here,' she told him, hoping her face wasn't as red as it felt. Her skin was vibrating with energy and she felt like she had the strength to lift the whole ship. She needed to do something, burn off the energy. She avoided looking at Phyleus as Epizon nodded thanks at her and lowered himself slowly into the captain's chair.

'I might do a few laps around the deck,' she said, flexing her fists.

Epizon laughed.

'Save your energy. See what Ares is about to say. You might need to give the ship a boost.'

Gods, she hoped not. She didn't trust her control just now.

'Cap,' said Abderos, rolling onto the quarterdeck with Len at his side.

'Abderos,' she answered, the sight of him bringing her back to reality a little. 'How are you feeling about going to Aries? We'll make sure you stay on the ship if it's possible.'

'To be honest with you, Cap, the gladiator pits are nothing compared to these Trials.' He shrugged as he said it but his eyes were dark.

'Hopefully the Trial will have nothing to do with the pits. There are many tribes and regions on Aries,' Epizon said.

'The giants should do well in this one. They all live on Aries,' said Phyleus.

'Yeah. Well, them or Theseus, as long as it's not Hercules,' Lyssa said.

'We will win on Aries,' said Nestor, hooves clicking as she came up the slope to the quarterdeck. 'We are all warriors.'

The flames crackled loudly over their conversation and they all turned to the dish as Ares appeared, large and looming in the fire, his face covered with his shining helmet.

'Heroes. You will journey to the southernmost tip of my realm, to Themiscyra. There Hippolyta, Queen of the Amazons, will receive you. Your task is to win her magic belt, imbued with her tribe's fierce strength. She will host a tournament of three tests, one of strength, one of speed and one of skill. A different crew member must perform each. The games start as soon as you all arrive.' The god vanished from the flames without another word.

'Well, that seems simple enough. Who wants to be involved?' said Lyssa, turning to her crew. 'Unfortunately Ep, you're going to have to...' She froze mid-sentence when she saw his face. He was pale again and staring slack-jawed at the fire dish. 'Epizon, what's wrong?'

'The Amazons...' he said quietly and looked at Lyssa. 'I never thought...'

Lyssa crouched down in front of him, concern over-riding her restlessness.

'Is it Tenebrae?' she asked.

Epizon shook his head.

'No. It's my mother.'

EVADNE

Evadne had always wanted to visit Aries. The crescent-shaped island was notoriously dangerous and that in itself had been enough to fascinate her. Not as much as the underwater world of Aquarius, but enough that her chest ached as they flew closer to the speck of land below them. Yet the excitement she longed for, the thrill of seeing such a land, of meeting a tribe like the Amazons, just wasn't there.

She groped for it, recalling the things she'd read about the secretive tribe of warrior women, fierce and strong. They didn't allow men to live among them. What would that be like? Evadne had never had female friends. She tucked a strand of her blue hair behind her ear as she leaned on the railings of the *Hybris*. She'd always told herself that other women didn't like her because they were jealous of her looks and intellect, or intimidated by her ambition and forwardness. But now she knew that wasn't true. The lonely, bitter child in her had deliberately kept her alone. She'd honed her standoffish attitude, reserving it for girls she saw as a threat to her own progression, and turning on her charm for men who could further her cause.

And now she didn't even know what her cause was worth. Immortality. The ultimate fame and fortune. For what? She would still be alone, friendless and fearful of her captain. She stared down at the ocean, watching Aries grow larger, rocky cliffs faintly discernible at the island's edge. She wanted to talk to Eryx. She needed him to know she wasn't like Hercules. He was the closest thing to a friend she had and he thought she was a monster.

Suddenly she found thinking of him unbearable. Anger filled her, and though Hercules's face filled her mind, nausea twisted her gut as she thought about aiming that crossbow at Lyssa. The overwhelming hatred was for herself, she realised. She needed someone to know she was sorry. She needed to say the words aloud, absolve herself of the brutality that could have overcome her. And it had to be Eryx who heard her say it. He had to believe she could be saved.

'Evadne.' Hercules's voice made her jump and she spun around, heart hammering.

'Captain.'

He walked across the deck towards her, his huge boots thudding on the planks. He wore his lion-skin cloak over his shoulders and *Keravnos* was strapped to his belt. He was ready for action.

'You will be taking the skill test.'

She blinked at him.

'There's no choice. I must take the strength test and Asterion is much faster than you.'

'Right. Of course, Captain,' she said. He was talking about the Trial. She had to take part in it.

Abderos's broken body lying amongst the vicious mares flashed in her mind. If this Trial was a dangerous as the last, her worries about the future might be for nothing.

IT TOOK another hour for the *Hybris* to reach Themiscyra, most of which Evadne spent fighting her growing self-hatred and trying to work out what skill she might be tested on. She felt no more prepared, though, as the ship descended gently alongside a rocky cliff that dropped straight into the ocean. Lining the clifftop, running all the way around the southern peninsula of the island, was what had looked like a stone wall from a distance but was actually a building, with windows and ledges lining both the cliff- and the desert-facing sides. A series of long piers ran out from the cliff wall and Hercules expertly manoeuvred the ship so that its deck lined up perfectly with an empty pier. The only other ship Evadne could see was the shabby *Alastor*. She glanced at Hercules but he said nothing.

'CAPTAIN HERCULES,' called a female voice as they came to a stop. Hercules climbed quickly down the stairs from the quarterdeck and Evadne hurried after him. Asterion was waiting by the mast and fell in behind them both as they approached the railings.

Two women were standing on the pier, waiting. They were wearing brown material strapped over their chests with coarse ropes, and had similar skirts tied around their waists, their stomachs bare and rippling with muscle. Metal guards were secured around their wrists and they had long leather boots laced up to their knees. Both had blond hair pushed back from their tanned skin by heavy-looking metal headguards.

'Queen Hippolyta welcomes you to Themiscyra. Please follow us,' one of the women said, gesturing towards the clifftop structure with the long wooden spear she was holding.

'I look forward to meeting her,' said Hercules, and vaulted over the railings. Evadne and Asterion followed him over the edge of the ship and their guides turned and set off up the pier. Evadne couldn't help gaping at how muscular the two women's broad shoulders were as she walked behind them. She wondered if these women had been chosen deliberately, to be intimidating, or whether all Amazons were like that.

She got her answer quickly.

As they reached the building, Evadne saw that most of the bottom floor was made up of arched tunnels, leading straight through. They entered the closest one, dark and cool inside, then her eyebrows shot up as they emerged on the other side. She had expected barren desert beyond, but she found herself in an earth-floored courtyard, surrounded by lush green trees. More stone archways jutted out of the building, vines with brightly coloured flowers wrapping around them. Their guides turned left and they followed, walking through another connected courtyard that hugged the main building. This one was filled with women, identically dressed, throwing spears at targets, wrestling on the ground or standing in lines, kicking and punching the air to shouted commands.

They walked straight through the middle of the training

ground, and Hercules kept his gaze fixed ahead. Evadne tried to copy him, but she couldn't, her eyes drawn instead to the activity around her. Every single woman Evadne could see was immeasurably stronger, harder and fiercer than she could ever hope to be. As nervous as they made her, she felt awestruck watching them. A woman with deep brown skin roared as she loosed a spear, her eyes narrowed and sharp. Her expression didn't change as it thudded into the centre of a disc hanging against a tree thirty feet away, and Evadne raised her eyebrows as she dropped into a crouch, than sprang forward, covering half the distance in one leap and landing running. The Amazon flew at the tree, wrenching the spear out of the wood and streaking towards another target in the next tree without slowing.

Evadne let out a long breath. If her skill test was to be against a woman like that then she stood no chance of winning.

8

HEDONE

Relief and excitement pulsed through Hedone as she saw the *Hybris*, moored at the next pier over. He was here. She would see her love soon enough.

The giants were mooring on the other side of them, proving how agonisingly slowly they had made their way to Aries. Theseus had insisted they take the maximum time they could to rest, as the Trial couldn't start until they were all there. Hedone knew it was just to keep her away from Hercules as long as possible. She'd barely spoken a word to either Theseus or Psyche since their fight.

'Which test would you like to do?' asked Theseus, coming to stand beside her as the ship stopped. Two women dressed in ropes and rags were standing on the pier, and Hedone frowned at them. They were armed with spears and looked even stronger than Psyche.

'Whichever.' She shrugged.

'Hedone, please.'

She sighed.

'Not the strength one.'

'You're decent with a spear now and you can run fast, so either skill or speed would suit you. You choose,' he said.

'Speed,' she said. She didn't care. She wasn't staying on this ship. She wasn't planning to compete at all.

'CAPTAIN THESEUS. Queen Hippolyta welcomes you to Themiscyra. Please follow us,' one of the women said. Her hard face softened as she smiled at Theseus, and Hedone barely stopped herself from rolling her eyes. They all thought he was so perfect. So beautiful and wise and kind. They were all idiots. He was as selfish and vain as everyone else.

They walked in silence up the pier and through the long cliff building. Hedone expected to see desert on the other side, but the passageway led to lush gardens. There were women dressed in little more than scraps of fabric and metal armour everywhere she looked. She'd grown up in a temple surrounded by women, albeit significantly more gentle ones than these seemed to be, and she stared around in fascination.

'Men are not allowed to live among the Amazons,' Theseus said quietly. Hedone didn't mean to respond but his words surprised her.

'No men? What about love? Pleasure?'

'Not all women need men for that, you know,' snapped Psyche.

Hedone scowled at her.

'I'm well aware of that. But most do.'

'Love makes warriors weak,' Theseus said as they approached a long, glittering pool. Water flowed into it from a huge statue of a minotaur tipping a large jug, standing at the far end. An ancient-style building with no walls, the roof held up by ornate columns, occupied the area behind the pool. It was filled with daybeds covered in plush, bright cushions. Women lounged on the beds, eating and drinking.

'Love gives warriors something to fight for. It makes them stronger,' said Hedone quietly.

'No. It gives them something to fear,' replied Psyche. 'It gives their enemies something to use.'

Anger rose in Hedone at his words. She would make Hercules stronger, not weaker. He would fight harder knowing she was there for him, that he had something to live for. She gritted her teeth and pushed her chin out, determined not to waste her words on these fools. They didn't understand.

They veered left, to walk around the pool, and as they got closer to the building she saw him. He was sitting on one of the daybeds, his lion skin wrapped around his hulking shoulders, a stern expression on his beautiful face. As if he knew she was there, he turned around and their eyes locked. There was no doubt in her mind. He knew her. He loved her. She wouldn't be apart from him any more.

The tribe of Amazons were not a polite or gentle people. Rather they were aggressive and brutal and were mostly driven by a need for war. But war ran in their veins, as they were daughters of Ares and the nymph Harmonia; who lay with him in the woods, then gave birth to girls who fell in love not with men, but with fighting.

EXCERPT FROM

ARGONAUTICA BY APOLLONIUS RHODIUS

Written 3 BC

Paraphrased by Eliza Raine

9

LYSSA

The last thing Lyssa had expected Epizon to say was the word 'mother'. She sat back and stared at him. 'Your mother?'

He closed his eyes and took a long breath.

'The Amazons are such a secretive tribe I never thought for a minute that the Trial would involve them.'

'Your mother is from Themiscyra?' Len's voice rang with shock.

'Yes.'

'Forgive my ignorance, but why is that so shocking?' asked Phyleus hesitantly.

Epizon looked at him.

'The Amazon warriors are all women, and men are not allowed to live amongst them. In order to continue their tribe they are allowed to visit with the nearby Gargarean people once a year. If an Amazon falls pregnant and the baby is a girl, then the tribe celebrates, and keeps the child. If the baby is born a boy then they either send the child back to the father, or kill it.' Lyssa swallowed a choke of protest. 'When I was born, by the colour of my skin it was obvious I was not a child of a Gargarean. My mother was exiled and we lived like nomads in the south of Aries. She fought, in the pits, in arranged matches, wherever she could, to win lodging or food. She... she kept me alive but even as an infant I knew she was repulsed by me. When I was five, she competed in a gladiator trial and an Amazonian chief was watching. She was so impressed with my mother's skill that she offered her a chance to repent, and re-join her tribe. The price was leaving me behind. She sold me to the pits and left that day.'

'Ep...' Lyssa whispered, laying her hand on his massive leg. 'I'm sorry.'

'I did well in the pits, and became sought after. I was sold from slaver to slaver for years, and when I became a man, the slavers began talking to courtesans. I'd grown up fighting, never questioned it, but the idea of being sold for love... I couldn't do it. I escaped and talked my way onto the first ship I could find leaving Aries.'

'Did you ever find out who your father was?'

'No.'

'Does anyone on this ship *not* have really shit parents?' Phyleus said, frowning.

'Mine are all right,' said Abderos.

'Never met mine,' grunted Len.

'Mine are magnificent,' said Nestor.

'Course they are.' Len rolled his eyes.

'Ep, you can't fight yet, so there's no reason for you to leave the ship. You won't have to see her,' Lyssa said.

'I would have loved the chance to fight in front of her,' he said, his eyes meeting Lyssa's. She gripped his leg harder.

'To show her she was right to keep me alive.' Her heart ached for him.

'You owe her nothing, Ep.'

He frowned, shaking his head.

'It's their way, Lyssa. She should have killed me the day I was born. But she didn't.'

Lyssa raised her eyebrows sceptically.

'Captain Lyssa!' A female voice rang across the deck and Nestor trotted to the railings.

'An escort is here,' she said.

'I'm sorry, Epizon. We have to go.' She pushed herself to her feet, reluctant to let go of her best friend.

'I'm sorry I can't help,' he said, his face pinched. 'Good luck.'

'I want to do the speed test,' said Nestor.

'Nestor, if it's not on land then you're not the best option. You can't swim,' Lyssa replied, turning to the centaur.

'The skill test, then,' she said, tail flicking but face unmoving.

'Fine.'

'I'll do the speed test,' Phyleus said. She nodded at him.

'Let's go.'

10

EVADNE

E vadne struggled not to react as Lyssa arrived at the building by the pool, accompanied by Phyleus and the white-haired centaur. The look she gave Hercules was so loaded with venom, she thought that Lyssa might launch herself at him and finish what they'd started by the stables. But a loud gong sounded, and everybody's attention was drawn to the empty desert beyond the open-walled building.

Approaching across the sand was a woman, dressed in the same style as the others, but with red painted in slashes across the fabric. Her blond hair was cropped short and she carried a gleaming war-hammer. As she got close, Evadne's breath caught. Her eyes were as blue as those of the giants, shining in the bright light. Full lips were quirked in a half-smile as she swung the hammer. With the exception of Aphrodite, she was the most impressive, captivating woman Evadne had ever seen. Even more than Hedone.

Evadne turned, looking sideways at her captain. Hercules was watching the woman climb the steps to the building, his expression hard and cold.

'Heroes,' she said, reaching the daybeds. All of the Amazon women in the building slid from their beds, bending one knee. Theseus and Busiris did the same, and slowly the rest of the crews followed suit. All except Hercules, who remained sitting on a purple cushion. 'Thank you,' she said as they stood up again. 'I am Queen Hippolyta. Welcome to Themiscyra. Enjoy your time here, as you will never see it again.' She smiled around at them, her gaze lingering on Theseus. 'We do not normally let strangers into this place, and rarer still is the presence of a man. There are rules that must be obeyed. The gardens are yours to explore as you wish. This building is a cabana. You each have one of your own to use as your base while you are here. There will be food and drink in them, and they are located on the desert edge so they are quiet for you to rest in. This is the limit of my hospitality.' Her eyes were as sharp as her voice. 'My warriors will not want to speak to you. Do not try. Ask an escort or serving girl if you need something. Now. Let us begin the first test with no further delay. I hope you've all brought a decent archer.' She quirked an eyebrow, twirling her hammer like it weighed nothing. 'Follow me,' she said, and turned, jumping down the steps and striding away across the dusty sand.

HERCULES STOOD UP LANGUIDLY, and Evadne tensed, rocking on her booted heels, itching to follow after Hippolyta. She said nothing, though, waiting for Hercules to move first, then falling in behind him.

They walked for ten minutes or so across the hot sand, away from the gardens, before she saw a new stone building ahead. It was semi-circular and had rows and rows of stepped benches surrounding a round stage area in the middle, a lot like the gladiator pit made from ice on Capricorn, but cut in half. The benches were filled with people, mostly Amazons, but not all. There were men, giants, harpies, minotaurs, and many other creatures besides. Massive green plants grew up and over the back of the stone and their huge leaves formed shady canopies that covered the seats. Evadne could hear the low rumble of the giants talking ahead of her, and wished she was talking to somebody, to distract her from her nerves. Talking to Eryx.

THE EXCITED HUM of the spectators rose in volume as they reached the building, and Hippolyta stopped and turned to them.

'This is your stadium, heroes. It is called the Colosseum. Put forward your crew member with the best aim now. Others, take a seat.' She gestured with her hammer at the bottom row of benches.

'Evadne, go,' said Hercules, and without looking at her he made his way across the empty stage towards the seats.

She looked around at the other crews. It looked like the centaur was staying, as were Theseus and Busiris. When everyone else had taken a seat, Hippolyta held up her hammer and the crowd immediately fell silent. A shiver of anticipation, and not a little fear, rippled through Evadne. Four Amazon warrior women stepped onto the stage, all carrying two bows each. They were long, curved bows, nothing like the ones Evadne was used to.

'You will each take a turn with one of my warriors,' said Hippolyta, into the silence. 'You will stand thirty feet apart, facing each other. They will fire at you first. You will fire at a target board. If you hit the target, the arrow fired at you will be destroyed. If you miss, the arrow will continue on its path, and my archers never miss. Three arrows each. Closest to the centre of the target wins. Or the last one left standing.' She winked at Theseus. 'Understood?' She looked at each of them in turn. Evadne nodded as the woman's piercing blue eyes fell on her.

'Let the games begin!' she roared, swinging her hammer down, then sprinting across the stage towards the crowd. One of the four archers walked towards them and held a bow out to Theseus. He took it and followed her pointed arm to a red cross painted on the stone ground of the stage. When he reached it, she stood on the opposite cross and another warrior rolled a target board mounted on wheels into the middle of the stage between them. Evadne gulped, fear pooling in her stomach. The target was barely bigger than her head.

'Ready?' called the archer, drawing her bow, arrow already notched. Theseus lifted his bow, carefully pulling the string back, arrow balanced.

'Yes,' he called.

The word had barely left his mouth when the archer loosed her arrow. It flew from her bow, its shining silver tip whistling through the air. Theseus loosed his own arrow and Evadne watched, wide-eyed as it thunked into the target. The Amazon's arrow gave a small pop, and exploded, a small shower of light sparking from it. The crowd roared, clapping and cheering.

'Ready?' Evadne heard the archer call over their noise. Theseus notched another arrow and pulled the bow up quickly.

'Ye—' This time he didn't even finish the word before she loosed her own arrow. He fired back almost too late, and although he hit the target the arrow was only inches from his head when it exploded, making him leap back. This time the crowd erupted into laughter. Evadne's stomach started to churn, anxiety gripping her. The Amazon archers were so fast, the target so small. What if she missed?

Theseus wasted no time notching his final arrow, and had the bow lifted to his face when the archer called 'Ready?' for the third time. And he hit the target in plenty of time, her arrow exploding harmlessly over the stage. He gave the cheering crowd a wave as he handed the bow back to the archer and walked to the bench to sit with Psyche and Hedone.

The next archer came forward, holding a bow out to the centaur this time. Nestor took it, trotting gracefully up to the red cross. She notched her arrow and aimed quickly, much more quickly than Theseus first had.

'Ready?' called the second archer, a smaller woman than the first, with long dark hair.

'Yes!' shouted Nestor. They loosed their arrows at almost the same time, Nestor's flying easily towards the target. When the archer's arrow exploded, the sparks were red and the crowd hollered and stamped.

Evadne squinted at the target. Nestor's arrow had hit the middle of the circle painted on the board. The anxiety crept further over her skin as the centaur reloaded her bow lightning fast. Evadne was never going to win.

11

ERYX

Eryx tried to remain calm as he watched the centaur sink her third arrow into the target, almost touching the previous two. There was no contest. She wouldn't be beaten. So did Busiris and Evadne really have to take their turns? He wasn't overly bothered about Busiris getting hurt but he had no wish to see harm come to Evadne.

Nestor trotted back to her crew a few seats over from where he and Antaeus were sitting, Lyssa standing and waving her arms in delight. The third archer walked out, handing a larger than normal bow to Busiris, who towered over her. He took it, testing its string as he walked to the cross. Another warrior ran out and adjusted the target, making it a few feet higher. Antaeus grunted his approval beside him. Eryx was glad he was doing the speed test. He would have been terrible at this. Although he didn't recall Busiris being particularly good at archery. It wasn't a skill giants practised much.

The lithe blond archer drew back her loaded bow and called, 'Ready?'

The crowd fell silent again as Busiris raised his own bow.

'Yes,' he called back, and her arrow flew towards him. Busiris let his own go slowly, and Eryx winced as it clipped the side of the target and the speeding arrow exploded inches from Busiris's gold face. He barely ducked out of the way of the sparks in time.

'He needs to be faster than that,' murmured Antaeus.

'Definitely,' Eryx agreed, hardly audible over the laughing crowd. Busiris didn't reload any faster, though and was still trying to balance his arrow when the girl raised her bow.

'Ready?' she called. There was an awkward pause while Busiris fumbled with the weapon, and snickers began rippling through the watchers.

'Yes,' he called eventually, and mercifully loosed his own arrow quickly. To Eryx's surprise it landed fairly centrally on the target and the Amazon's arrow exploded safely. She had reloaded and was aiming at him within a few seconds. A slow chant started up through the crowd as Busiris fought with his third arrow.

'*Ittiménos, Ittiménos,*' the spectators chanted. Busiris looked around at them all, teeth bared. Eryx knew the word, had had it chanted at him in boxing matches many times. *Loser.* Years of fighting had taught him how to ignore the crowd, how to focus. Years of experience Busiris didn't have.

'Ready?' the archer called.

'Yes,' Busiris ground out, but it was clear he hadn't got his bow up fully. Her arrow loosed, and Eryx scowled as Busiris let his fly late, and low. Antaeus half stood up as Busiris's arrow missed the target completely, clattering across the sandy ground.

'Move!' Antaeus roared as Busiris stared dumbly at the

archer's arrow flying towards him. He leaped to the side, but he was too late, and bellowed in pain as the arrow tore across his cheek. Bright red blood swelled slowly in a line across his face, all the way to his ear, then began to drip down his cheek. He pressed his hands to the side of his face.

'My ear!' he shouted, stumbling towards Antaeus. Eryx winced.

'My medics will attend you.' Hippolyta's voice boomed across the stadium. Three smaller women, in white robes, stood up from their seats a few rows back, and made their way towards him. Eryx looked at Evadne, now standing alone on the other side of the stage, framed by the barren desert. She was staring at the blood on the ground by the red cross, her face pale. An overwhelming urge to comfort her overtook him and he clenched his fists in his lap. There was nothing he could do but watch.

As THE MEDICS led the wailing half-giant away, the last archer handed a bow to Evadne. She took it, and strode to the cross, chin pushed out, blue hair swinging in a high ponytail. Pride filled Eryx and he shuffled forward in his seat. She notched and drew quickly, and was ready when the archer called out to her. Her first arrow thudded into the target, well off centre but in plenty of time for the Amazon's arrow to explode harmlessly. Eryx took a deep breath as she quickly reloaded, giving the crowd no time to put her off.

'Ready?' called the archer.

'Yes.' Her voice sounded small in the large arena. Her second arrow missed the target. For a second Eryx was sure his heart had stopped beating, as Evadne froze, bow still in place. Then she dropped to the ground, throwing her body forward and flinging the bow away. The arrow exploded as it hit the red cross, and Evadne scrambled awkwardly back to her feet a short distance away, panting. The crowd whooped and cheered, the odd booing sound mingling with the celebration. Eryx realised his palms were sweating as he flexed his tense fists.

Evadne bent to retrieve her bow, and it was clear her hands were shaking. She would never hit the target now. Eryx leaned forward as she planted her feet back on the cross and drew the loaded bow back for the last time.

'Ready?'

'Yes.' She loosed immediately, and blessed relief swamped Eryx as Evadne's arrow hit the target. She sagged as the archer's arrow exploded, dropping the bow to the ground and turning towards the crowd. But instead of looking at her own crew, at Hercules, her eyes found Eryx's. He stared, the sounds of the crowd dimming to nothing as her frightened, intense gaze bored into his.

12

HERCULES

Hercules said nothing as Hippolyta pronounced Nestor the winner of the skill test and told them they had two hours until the strength test. He said nothing when Evadne apologised to him, over and over again, as they were escorted to their own daybed-filled building for rest and refreshments. He said nothing until their escorts left and he was alone with Evadne and Asterion.

'WHAT IN ZEUS'S name did you think you were doing?' he bellowed at the idiot girl. 'All you had to do was hit a target! Everyone else hit the middle!'

He raised his hand as he stepped towards her and she darted backwards, falling onto a cushioned bed. 'You won't avoid me this time, Evadne,' he hissed. And she wouldn't. He'd had enough. Enough of watching others claim his glory, of watching others get chances he didn't, of watching others being aided by those stronger than they were. 'Why did I end up with you? Lyssa gets a fighter, a centaur, a prince. Theseus gets the demi-goddess of pleasure, Antaeus gets a crew of inhumanly strong giants, and me? Why did I end up with a pathetic, useless, weak little girl that I can't even bear to look at any more?' he hissed.

She didn't look up at him, but tears streamed down her face. Satisfaction and desire pulsed through him. He would make her pay for embarrassing him one too many times.

'HERCULES,' a woman's voice said. He turned around slowly, dropping his raised arm when he saw Hippolyta. She held out a jug to him as she stepped into the cabana. 'Wine?'

He took a deep breath, and straightened up. She was a handsome woman, of that there was no doubt. But she paled in comparison to Hedone.

'There are glasses behind you,' said Hippolyta. Asterion hurried forward, lifting an ornate crystal glass from a table amongst the beds. 'I'll have one too,' she said to the minotaur. He bowed his head and picked up another quickly, trotting over with them both.

'Thank you,' Hercules said formally as Hippolyta reached him, then filled their glasses.

'You know, I've seen few avoid an arrow as quickly as you did then,' she said, and turned to Evadne. Hercules looked at the girl, still sitting on the bed, shaking. She just stared silently at Hippolyta, tears still rolling down her face. Coiled energy pounded through his body. 'You did well,' the woman said, and took her own glass to Evadne. Anger gripped Hercules as Hippolyta crouched in front of her.

'Drink it. You will feel better,' she said softly. Evadne took the glass, and drained it immediately.

'You have no right—' started Hercules, but the woman cut him off, standing up quickly.

'I have every right,' she snarled, advancing on him. 'I am queen here, and what I say is final. If you lay a hand on that girl while you are here in Themiscyra, I will kill you myself.'

Rage hammered through Hercules, his muscles tensing and swelling with power. He took a step towards her. She may look strong for a woman, but she was still just that.

'I'd love to see you try,' he hissed.

Hippolyta barked a laugh and put both her hands on her hips.

'Very well, mighty Hercules. I shall see you in the ring in two hours.' She whirled around, stamping down the steps from the building. Hercules glared after her, his face twitching in fury.

'If she wants to show her tribe how weak she is, then so be it,' he growled.

13

LYSSA

'Nestor, I had no idea you were such a good shot!' Phyleus ginned up at the centaur.

'My aim is as good as many others'; the difference is my ability to remain unaffected by pressure,' she said simply.

'Well, you did great,' said Lyssa, taking a swig of the wine that had been on the little table among the daybeds.

'What do you think you'll have to do for the strength test?' Phyleus asked her.

She shrugged. 'Lift stuff? Or fight,' she said.

'What are you hoping for?'

Lyssa cocked her head, thinking.

'There's nothing I can lift that Hercules can't. So a fight, I guess.'

'Do you need me to annoy you? Get the Rage going?' Phyleus eyes were sparkling with mischief as he spoke.

'You don't have to annoy me, you know,' she replied to him in her head. 'There are other ways you can make me strong.'

She watched with satisfaction as his eyes widened, his cheeks tingeing with pink.

'Just say the word, Captain,' he replied silently. 'I'm yours to command.'

She watched his lips part slightly, and felt her skin hum to life.

'I don't believe you need me here, Captain,' said Nestor, and Lyssa's gaze snapped guiltily to the centaur. 'Do you mind if I speak with the Amazons? Artemis has many questions for them.'

'No, no, of course not, as long as Hippolyta doesn't mind,' she answered.

Nestor bowed her head, then trotted down the steps from the cabana building, towards the training courtyard.

As soon as the centaur was out of sight, Phyleus got up from the daybed he was sitting on, reaching Lyssa's in a few short strides. Anticipation shot through her, like electricity, her fingertips and toes tingling. How did he cause such a reaction in her? And why had she resisted it for so long? She grabbed the front of his shirt as he reached her, pulling him down onto the bed beside her. He let out a gasp of surprise, then laughed as he reached for her. Their lips met, and power thrummed through Lyssa, every nerve in her body tingling. It was so much like the Rage, the unreleased power, the bottomless energy, the feeling of limitlessness. She kissed him harder, and he responded, pushing his hands into her hair, pulling her closer to him. She couldn't get enough of him, she wanted everything he had to give her, and her brain was fogging over, unable to think about anything else.

'Lyssa,' he said, pulling away from her slightly, to look at her.

'What?' she breathed.

'You know we can't... You know. Go further than kissing. Not here.'

She stared at him, trying to understand his words through her haze of desire.

'Yeah,' she said eventually. He grinned at her.

'Gods, I want you. But we have to wait.' He kissed her bottom lip, gently, and pulses of power rippled through her body with each touch.

'Wait,' she repeated. She didn't want to wait. But he was right. And she wasn't about to let him do all the teasing. 'Course. This is all just to get my power going.' She was still gripping the front of his shirt with one hand, and she let go, but pushed him back, until he was lying on the bed. He took a slow breath in and she ran a finger down his neck, over his throat and down the middle of his chest, until his shirt prevented her going further. The tiny hairs on his skin rose up, and she felt his shudder.

'Is it working?' he asked.

'Yes,' she whispered, and leaned over to kiss him again.

14

EVADNE

Mercifully, Hercules had ignored Evadne since Hippolyta's visit. She still hadn't stopped shaking, though. She couldn't work out if it was dodging the arrow, or Hercules's raised fist that was causing her body to react so physically. She wanted more of the wine the Amazon queen had given her, but the decanter was on the table next to Hercules and she daren't go near him. He was drinking and staring into space. Asterion sat silently nearby. It felt like an age before the escorts came back.

'Are you ready for the next test?' a blond warrior asked.

Hercules stood up immediately.

'Let's go,' he barked.

Evadne got up quickly, and Asterion did the same. They walked from the cabana, across the dusty sand until they reached the Colosseum again. Busiris's blood was gone from the red cross, but the rows of seats were still filled with spectators, who roared and stamped and booed as they approached.

In his lion skin, Hercules was easily distinguishable from the others. His face creased into a snarl and Evadne instinctively fell further behind him, where he couldn't see her.

'They have heard about your challenge of our queen,' one of the escorts said, without turning or breaking stride. 'We love our queen, very much. None who have challenged her have won.'

Hercules didn't respond, but shook off the lion-skin cloak. He was shirtless beneath, and as Evadne stared at her captain's back, rippling with tense muscles, she realised that she didn't want him to win. She didn't want to be anywhere near him if he lost, but she wanted the fierce Hippolyta to beat him. Immortality be damned, Hercules deserved to lose.

IT WAS a relief to leave the side of the stage this time, as she and the minotaur made their way to the bottom row of seats. She looked hopefully for Eryx, but he had Busiris, his head and ear wrapped in a dressing, to one side of him, and a whole row of people on his other side. She walked awkwardly along the bench, looking for an empty spot.

'Here,' someone called, and she looked over to see Theseus shuffling along, trying to make a space for her. Hedone, sitting on the other side of him, scowled. 'Evadne. Sit here.' The Amazon sitting beside the narrow open space sighed and moved down too, so that there was enough room to sit. Evadne did.

'Thanks,' she mumbled, looking out at the stage. Lyssa, Psyche and Antaeus were hovering around the edge of the dusty circle, well apart from Hercules.

'No problem,' Theseus replied. 'You did well, last test.' She looked sideways at him, cautious. Why was he being nice to her?

The crowd suddenly leaped to their feet as one, shouting and cheering as Hippolyta walked into view. She raised her arms as she reached the centre of the stage, and everyone fell silent.

'The second test is one of strength,' she called, her voice echoing around the stone structure. 'And here in Themiscyra there's no better way to test one's strength than with a fist fight. No weapons allowed. The first to get one of my warriors to yield will win. If none of you can do so, then the winner will be the last one left alive. Captain Hercules has asked specifically to fight me.' A massive cheer went up from the watchers. Surely Queen Hippolyta would never yield, Evadne thought, slight panic rippling through her. If she was not stronger than Hercules, then she would die. And how could she be? He had the strength of the lord of the gods.

'Ares versus Zeus. This should be good,' Theseus said, leaning forward. He said it casually, but the muscles in his neck were straining, and the easy glimmer he usually had in his eyes was absent.

'What do you mean?'

'Son of Zeus against daughter of Ares. They will be well matched. Hercules was a fool to bait her; anyone else might have been an easy win for him.'

'Hippolyta is the daughter of Ares?'

'Sure.' Theseus looked at her. 'Did you think she was just a human? Look at her!'

Evadne flushed as she watched Hippolyta line up with three other Amazon warriors on the stage, gesturing for Hercules to stand opposite her.

'There's not a lot about the Amazons in any of my books,' Evadne said defensively.

'No, I guess there wouldn't be,' Theseus replied, eyes still fixed on the Queen.

'How do you know so much about them?' Evadne asked.

He glanced at her.

'I have access to information,' he said dismissively.

'Aphrodite told you?'

'Yeah.'

Evadne was sure he was lying. Did it matter?

'Are you worried about Psyche?' she asked him quietly, watching as the woman removed her gleaming golden armour, then took up a place opposite a young blond Amazon.

Theseus turned to her with a smile.

'No. My first mate is a fair and fierce fighter. She'll yield if she needs to. Or she will win.'

Evade nodded.

'Hercules will win,' said Hedone, from his other side. Evadne saw Theseus flinch slightly, but he said nothing. So he *did* know about the two of them. That was interesting.

'It's anyone's fight. Antaeus has the advantage of size, and Lyssa is probably still furious about Abderos.'

'Hercules will win,' the beautiful woman repeated, staring at the stage. Evadne followed her gaze. Antaeus towered over his opponent, a dark-skinned woman who was a foot taller than most of the other Amazons, but still a long way off the giant's full height. Lyssa was opposite a slight olive-skinned girl, well matched to her size. If Lyssa was half as angry as she'd been when she'd wielded *Keravnos* outside the stables, the girl didn't stand a chance.

'Are you ready?' Hippolyta's voice boomed through the stadium. All the other fighters in the ring nodded. They were all shifting from foot to foot, their nervous energy infectious. Hippolyta and Hercules were closest to the crowd, Antaeus the furthest away.

'Go!' the Queen shouted. Lyssa moved first, her red hair catching Evadne's eye as she flew at the girl facing her. The Amazon ducked, rolling under her blow and springing back to her feet behind Lyssa. A roar drew Evadne's attention to Hippolyta, who was beating her chest and advancing on the unmoving Hercules. He was half crouched, huge leg muscles bulging, ready to react. Evadne's eyes flicked to the giant, who was trying to flip his opponent off his back, but they were drawn straight back to the Queen.

Hippolyta's expression was filled with venom, her eyes wide and wild. Her mouth was open in a snarl and she drew both her arms back as she got within a foot of Hercules. He sprang at her and she hurled both fists forward with another roar. They caught him square in the chest and the man flew backwards, his whole body lifted from the ground. He crashed to the dirt, skidding towards Psyche and the blond fighter. Both women darted out of the way, barely taking their eyes off each other for a second. The crowd erupted into cheers and whoops, their excitement deafening.

Evadne realised she was holding her breath, and let it go slowly. There was no doubt about it, Hercules had underestimated his opponent.

Eryx shuffled forward on his seat, trying to concentrate on Antaeus. It was difficult, though. Between Hippolyta and Hercules throwing everything they had at each other, and his infuriatingly uncrushable desire to peer down the row of spectators, looking for Evadne, he was struggling to focus on his captain. Antaeus could win this, he was sure. The girl was half his size, and as long as he ended it quickly, he would come out on top. All boxers knew that. You don't give your opponent a chance to tire you out. Just end it quickly.

THE AMAZON HAD REPEATEDLY JUMPED onto his back, beating him across his ears and the side of his head exactly as Eryx himself did when he was fighting someone a lot larger than himself. Antaeus had managed to shake the girl off every time, but he'd so far failed to pin her down. She was lightning fast, and seemed to know exactly what he was about to do every time he moved. She was clearly an experienced fighter.

There was a collective intake of breath from the crowd and Eryx's eyes darted back across the stage. Hippolyta was on her hands and knees, Hercules bearing down on her. She dropped as he threw himself at the ground, his elbow ready to slam into her back, rolling out of his way just in time. There was an audible crack as his elbow hit the stone and Hippolyta had a vicious grin on her face as she sprang back to her feet, stamping at his head. He was as quick as she was, though, rolling away and pushing himself effortlessly into a crouch before her foot got near him.

Eryx continued to scan the stage. Psyche was rolling on the ground with her opponent, neither of them on the bottom of the tussle for long, before the other got the advantage back. They were well matched. Lyssa and the Amazon she was fighting were circling each other, tense and ready, a wary respect on both girls' faces.

A familiar bellow drew Eryx's attention back to Antaeus just in time for him to see the giant rip the Amazon woman from where she was wrapped around his shoulders by her neck. He held her flailing body out in front of him, her boots kicking above the ground.

'Yield!' he roared at her. She scratched and punched at the hand that gripped her, and he drew his arm back and slammed her to the ground, dropping to his knees and forcing his whole weight behind the movement. The stone gave a shuddering moan and the crowd fell silent as a choking voice coughed, 'I yield.'

'She yields!' shouted Antaeus, standing up and raising both his arms above his head. 'She yields!'

Hippolyta turned to look, and Hercules took his chance. The crowd exploded as he threw his fist at her turned head. Their warning gave her enough time to duck, but not enough to avoid the blow completely. She staggered sideways, and a triumphant expression spread across Hercules's face as her dazed eyes fell on him.

Then she moved so fast that neither Eryx nor any fighter in the world would ever have seen it coming. The dazed look fell away in a heartbeat, replaced by intense fury as her boot shot out. She kicked so high that she leaned sideways, her body dropping to accommodate the move, and Eryx flinched as her foot landed squarely against Hercules's throat. He gasped, choking, his hands flying to his neck, and she straightened up slowly.

'The fight was over, Hercules,' she said into the now-silent Colosseum. 'Antiope yielded. You will fight fair in Themiscyra or pay the price.' The huge man's eyes were streaming as he continued to choke for breath. She looked at Antaeus, who was pulling the tall Amazon warrior back to her feet. 'Congratulations, Captain Antaeus. You have won the strength Trial. I believe we could all do with a rest before we tackle speed. You will spend the night in Themiscyra. We will feast in the gardens tonight, and race tomorrow. Your cabanas are yours until then. Tralla, Thiba, Antiope, with me,' she said, looking at each of the three warriors in turn. They nodded and followed her as she strode from the stage without another look at Hercules.

THE CROWD BEGAN to clap and shout as Antaeus gave a victorious cheer and Eryx beamed at him. If he won the speed test tomorrow, they would win the Trial. And that would put them ahead of the others with only three Trials remaining.

But his smile slipped from his face as he saw Evadne and Asterion leave the benches, approaching Hercules. He threw a venomous look at them both, then stalked off the stage, still clutching his throat. Eryx heard a shout, then saw

Hedone yell something at Theseus, before running after Evadne and Asterion. Eryx frowned as he watched her run past the minotaur, and saw Evadne stop when she reached Hercules and began talking animatedly to him. Then Evadne turned around, and the fear on her face was clear even from this distance. Eryx half stood up, before remembering that he couldn't go to her. He *wouldn't* go to her. He dropped his gaze, unable to look at her. She had made her choice. She wasn't like him, or his crew.

'What's Hedone doing?' said Busiris beside him.

Eryx looked up again as they all began walking away, disappearing into the distance as they headed back towards the courtyards. He shrugged.

'Who cares. We won,' he said, but the words were less jubilant than they should have been.

16

HEDONE

Hedone said nothing as she walked beside Hercules. She was desperate to get back to the cabana, to be alone with him, so that he could drop his pride and let her help him. The minotaur and the blue-haired girl were trudging behind them, neither looking like they wanted to offer any help. Evadne seemed downright unsettled. Foolish girl. Hercules needed kindness and care, not immaturity. Each breath he took rattled in his throat and his face was red and tight. He'd not spoken a word as she'd run to him, asking him over and over what she could do to help. She knew he wouldn't show himself weak in front of people, though.

Finally they approached the cabana, and she rushed ahead to pour water for Hercules. He climbed the steps slowly, and sat down on the edge of one of the beds as he took the glass from her.

'Why don't you two go and... talk to the locals. Find out more about Themiscyra,' she said, looking up at Evadne and Asterion, hovering at the edge of the building.

'Captain?' said Asterion. Hercules nodded, the movement barely perceptible. Evadne turned away immediately, hurrying down the stone steps and out into the gardens without a word. Asterion's gruff face creased for a moment, then he left too, in the opposite direction to Evadne. Hedone sat down on the bed.

'Hercules,' she said softly, laying a hand on his leg. 'Hippolyta is a cruel woman, I don't know why she—' Hedone didn't finish the sentence, her words cut off as Hercules launched his glass across the cabana. It smashed against a stone column and he got to his feet, stalking over to the table of drinks. He poured wine into a taller glass, then gulped it down.

'She is a tool of Ares,' he croaked after his glass was drained. 'This is my father's battle, not mine.'

The sense of it struck Hedone.

'Of course...' she said slowly. 'Poor Hercules, always caught up in your father's actions.'

'Don't pity me, Hedone. I will show them. I will show them all that I am stronger.'

His words were hoarse and quiet, but the vitriol rang through regardless. He was angry. She had to make him feel better. She could feel his pain, his humiliation, deep inside her. She needed him to be happy.

'Let me help you,' she said quietly. He turned to her, the challenge in his fierce eyes dying away as she pulled the shoulder of her dress down. 'Let me help you in the best way I can, my love,' she said, pushing her power into her voice, seeing the effect of her seduction as his stance relaxed, and he stepped towards her. 'Let me take you away from all of this, for a while at least.' She tugged the other shoulder of her dress down and it dropped to the floor, pooling around her feet.

'Wait,' he said, dragging his gaze away from her body and up to meet hers. 'Does Theseus know you are here?'

She nodded.

'Yes. I told him yesterday that I am in love with you. I told him just now that I would be wherever you were, that you needed me and I needed you.' The words had been easy to say and now she was rewarded with the look on Hercules's face.

'Hedone, my love. You *are* strong. You are magnificent.'

'And I am yours.'

17

LYSSA

'I was this close!' exclaimed Lyssa for the tenth time since they'd returned to their cabana, falling back on a daybed and slamming her fists into the sumptuous pillows.

'Don't worry, we're still in the running. I'm not even sure why Hercules or Theseus would compete tomorrow. They can't win now,' Phyleus replied, handing her a glass of wine. Lyssa sat up to take the wine and drank deeply, still scowling.

'Maybe they won't,' said Nestor.

'Fine by me. Two less to worry about,' said Phyleus.

'Captain?' The voice in Lyssa's head took her by surprise.

'Epizon?' she answered aloud, sitting up straight.

'Captain, well done so far. I... I wonder if you could do me a favour.' He sounded nervous. She'd never heard her first mate nervous before.

'Of course, Ep. What's wrong?'

'The woman fighting Antaeus. The tall, dark-skinned woman. Antiope.'

'She's your mother.' As soon as Lyssa said the words, she

wondered how she hadn't realised it the moment she had seen her.

'Yes. Could you talk with her? As we're staying the evening now, I thought... I thought maybe she would like to meet with me.'

'Of course I will. I'll go and find her now.'

'Thank you, Captain.'

Lyssa looked at Phyleus and Nestor.

'How do we call those escorts?' she asked, setting her wine glass on the floor and standing up. She walked down the stone steps, towards the courtyards, looking for one of the younger girls who had brought them there. She could see nobody.

'Maybe you should go and find Antiope yourself?' Phyleus said.

'She might be with Hippolyta, though. And the Queen might not take kindly to the idea of one of her warriors meeting with her son.'

'True...'

'Although I'd love to thank her for what she did to Hercules.' Just thinking about the kick Hercules had taken to the throat made Lyssa feel stronger. Not only was he no closer to immortality, the world was being shown just how mortal he really was.

'Well, they'll probably be in the main palace. No harm in going for a little look.'

'There's plenty of harm in *you* going,' said Nestor.

'Me?' Phyleus frowned.

'Yes. You are a man. You will not be allowed anywhere inside the palace.'

'What about the feast? Tonight?'

'Hippolyta said it would be in the gardens.'

'Oh.'

Lyssa cocked her head at the disappointment on his face.

'Don't worry, *Prince* Phyleus,' she teased him. 'I'm sure there are plenty of places you can go that I can't.'

'And I'll take you to all of them, rules be damned.' He grinned at her.

A pulse of excitement shot through her. She believed him. He *would* take her anywhere. And she wanted to go with him. A warm feeling that she'd not felt in a long time spread through her chest as her mind raced, picturing them flying through the skies together, new places theirs to explore. The feeling was hope. Excitement about her future. Those lively, warm, beautiful eyes held the promise of a life she'd written off.

'I...' she started to say, but trailed off. He raised his eyebrows at her, in question.

'I want to go everywhere with you,' she said, in her mind.

A smile lit up his face, broad and true.

'Then that's where we'll go.'

Lyssa barely got through the first stone arch of the court-yards when a young girl, maybe twelve years of age, stopped her.

'Excuse me? Can I help you, Captain Lyssa?'

Lyssa smiled at her.

'I'm looking for Antiope. Can you take me to her?'

The girl stared at her for a moment, then said, 'Why do you want to see her? Is it about her losing today?'

Lyssa shook her head quickly.

'No, no, nothing like that. I... I know somebody from her past. I just wanted to talk to her about it.'

'Oh. Wait here, and I'll get her,' the girl said, pointing at a stone bench set opposite a series of mounted practice targets.

'Thank you,' Lyssa answered and sat down as the girl darted off. She was wearing the same coarse fabric tied with ropes that the warrior women did. What would it have been like to grow up here, Lyssa wondered. And did the women, the mothers, ever wonder about their discarded sons? She stood up again, reaching for the stack of bows by the bench. Why did these women refuse to live with men? She fished an arrow out of a shallow stone bowl on the ground and notched it, aiming at one of the targets. She loosed her arrow. It hit, but barely, right on the edge of the circle. Blowing out a sigh, she grabbed for another. She'd always been bad at archery. But practising hadn't appealed to her, when she could fight so well. Archery left her Rage unsatisfied.

She fired arrow after arrow, some hitting closer to the centre than others, but as many again completely missing the target.

'It's a good job you're practising,' said a disdainful voice behind her, as yet another arrow flew wide. She spun around, lowering the bow as she came face to face with Antiope.

'Hello,' she said, laying the weapon down on the bench.

'I'm told you wanted to see me?' the woman answered. She looked even fiercer this close than she had on the stage. Her skin was tanned, darker than many of the other Amazons, but nowhere near as dark as Epizon's. Her eyes were hard, and her mouth a straight line as she appraised Lyssa. Her biceps bulged as she folded her arms across her chest.

'Yes. I, er, I know someone from your past,' Lyssa said awkwardly.

'I doubt that,' Antiope said.

'He—' Lyssa started, but Antiope turned away.

'I have no interest in talking with you about any *man* from my past,' she spat as she took a long stride towards the palace.

'Even if he's your son?' Lyssa called after her.

Antiope froze, then turned back to her slowly.

'He lives?'

Lyssa nodded.

'He thrives. He is my first mate on the *Alastor*.' *Thrives* was a bit of an exaggeration, Lyssa thought, but she couldn't help bigging him up a bit.

'He serves under a woman?' Antiope said slowly.

'That surprises you?'

'A little. In my experience, the men who survive the Amazons grow to hate women.'

'Why do you hate men so much?' Lyssa couldn't help the question.

'They are unnecessary,' Antiope shrugged. 'Other than to procreate, of course.'

'What about love?' Phyleus's grinning face flashed in her mind as she said the word.

'My duty is enough for me. And I love my queen.'

Lyssa nodded. The Amazons were a war tribe of Aries. She supposed they wouldn't have survived if they could be distracted by emotions like love.

'Epizon would like to meet with you. While we are here.'

Antiope took a long breath, her face the most expressive Lyssa had seen it.

'Epizon? Is that his name now?'

Lyssa nodded.

'Why did he not come to Themiscyra and take part in the tests? Is he weak?'

'He is the strongest man on my ship, but he was gravely injured, by Hercules. I assume you've not been watching the Trials?'

'No. We have no interest in such things. Hippolyta only allowed all this to happen because Ares himself willed it.'

'Well, Epizon is recovering well now, but I had stronger crew-mates for the test.'

Antiope nodded.

'I understand. And I think I would like to meet him. But I will need to ask the permission of my queen.'

Lyssa's heart sank. Surely Hippolyta would not allow it.

'What do you think she will say?' she asked.

'I think she will say yes. I am her sister.'

'You're her sister?' Lyssa stared in surprise. 'So are you... a daughter of Ares too?'

'The families of the Amazons are complicated. Hippolyta has the true power of the god of war in her. I carry a fraction of that. But it is enough.' Her eyes were fierce again.

'I saw, today. I couldn't have fought a giant like that,' Lyssa said.

Antiope held her gaze for a moment.

'I have heard you are as strong as any Amazon, Captain Lyssa. I would like it very much if your father died.'

Lyssa blinked.

'So would I. And please don't call him my father.'

'Very well.' Antiope nodded. 'I will talk to Hippolyta and let you know her will presently.'

'Thank you,' said Lyssa, praying for Epizon's sake that the Queen would say yes.

18

ERYX

Eryx twirled the long, thin pasta around his spoon, watching the tomato sauce slide off in the warm glow of candlelight. He was sitting at a large, sturdy feasting table that filled one of the courtyards, and the light from the sky had grown dim enough that candles had been lit in lanterns everywhere.

'Why so glum, Brother?' asked Antaeus, slapping him hard on the back. 'Are you nervous about tomorrow?'

'No, of course not, Captain,' he answered, before shoving the food into his mouth.

'Good. You'll do great.' Antaeus beamed at him. He had drunk far more wine than he usually did, and Eryx suspected he was feeling the effects a little. He swallowed his pasta and smiled back.

'I know, Captain.'

'This is going to put us in the lead, Eryx. We're going to win!'

'Slow down, big man,' called Theseus from the other end of the table, with a laugh. 'You've got to beat Lyssa tomorrow before you can take the lead.'

'No, I haven't!' the giant exclaimed. 'Eryx has to beat the small, puny man!' He pointed at Phyleus, who was pulling apart a large lump of bread opposite them.

'Hey!' he said, looking up indignantly. Lyssa coughed back a laugh.

'He's very fast, Captain Antaeus. Eryx,' she said, looking at him, 'you'll have a real race on your hands.'

Eryx smiled weakly at her.

'Good,' he said.

'What's wrong with you? Looking for Evadne?' Busiris said quietly from his left. Trust that snake to notice he was preoccupied. He was right, though. None of Hercules's crew had arrived in the gardens for the feast. Nor had Hedone.

'What kind of race is it?' Psyche asked, turning to Hippolyta at the head of the table.

'I can't tell you that.' The Queen smiled, lifting a chicken leg off her loaded plate. 'Can I assume your Hedone will not be taking part, though?' The table fell quiet, everyone wanting to hear the answer.

'She's not *our* Hedone any more,' Psyche answered sharply.

'No, I'm afraid we will be withdrawing,' said Theseus more calmly.

'A shame, Captain Theseus,' Hippolyta said.

'You cannot control matters of the heart, my queen.' He shrugged, staring at her.

'Speak for yourself,' she answered, eyes sparkling, and bit into the leg of meat.

THESEUS'S WORDS rang through Eryx's mind, the rest of the banter around the table fading. *You cannot control matters of the heart.* Was that true? Was that why he couldn't stop thinking about her? He felt something flitting at his back and swatted at it absentmindedly. Then he felt it again, harder, and he turned, frowning in irritation. There, half-hidden in the lush plants surrounding their candlelit feasting table, was Evadne. She beckoned to him, then vanished into the greenery.

'I'm calling it a night, Captain,' he said, pushing his chair back as he stood up.

'Good idea. Get your rest, Eryx,' Antaeus said.

'Eryx, I'll see you tomorrow. May the best man win,' Phyleus said, and stood up too, extending his hand across the table. Eryx took it, surprised, dwarfing it in his own as he shook it.

'Tomorrow, Phyleus,' he said and turned towards where he had seen Evadne.

HE WANDERED through the gardens for five minutes or so before he found her, sitting on a stone bench. Her hair wasn't in its normal high tail but tied in a messy knot at her neck, and she was wearing trousers and a plain shirt instead of her usual tight clothes. She looked more beautiful than he had ever seen her.

'Eryx,' she said, standing up as she saw him. 'I'm really glad you came.'

'I shouldn't have,' he said gruffly. 'I meant what I said.'

'I know you did. And you were right.'

His eyebrows rose.

'I'm not playing games, Evadne.'

'I don't want to any more either. I swear. I didn't realise how far into one I was. Honestly. I... I didn't realise until I saw what he did to Abderos. I didn't realise how real the game had become.' She bit her lip as she spoke, wringing her hands. 'Eryx, I couldn't live with myself if I took a life,' she whispered. 'Hercules is a monster. And I'm not saying that he forced me to do anything, because he didn't but... I was so consumed by the thought of being famous, having people love me, care about me, that I... I lost sight of what it would cost to be like him.' She looked up at him. 'Can you forgive me?' she asked, her voice small.

Eryx hadn't expected to see her like this. The Evadne he was used to was tough, and sarcastic, and flirty and... not this. When he had followed her, he had thought she would argue with him, tell him to toughen up, to play the game. Had Abderos's death really made such a difference to her?

'Why? Why have you changed your mind? Do you not want immortality any more?'

'Of course I do. But not at that price. I saw Lyssa. I saw her grief. I don't want to make a person feel like that. Ever.' Some strength seeped into her voice. 'There's a better way to win. Your captain, and Theseus, they both care about their crew, and they won't kill to get ahead.'

'So she wants a different crew now?' Busiris's voice startled them both and Eryx spun around to see him approaching slowly through the gardens, the candlelight making his skin shine. 'And who can blame her, now that the lovely Hedone has replaced her?' he continued, his voice sickly-sweet. 'Poor Evadne. Hercules isn't going to pay you any attention now, is he? You probably won't last until the final Trial now that you've been replaced.'

'No, no, it's not like that!' she said, shaking her head. 'Eryx—'

Busiris cut her off. 'Eryx, she's using you. Again.'

'No!'

'She has no place on her crew now that her captain has a new pet, it's as simple as that.' Busiris's voice had turned hard and cold and he came to a stop next to Eryx.

'That's not true,' Evadne said, glaring at him.

'It's not true that you've been replaced? You think you'll be anything more than a servant to him now?' His mocking tone made Eryx want to hit him, but he couldn't help hearing the half-giant's words. He was right, it was a very convenient time for her to find her conscience.

'It's not true that that's the reason I wanted to talk. I just wanted... forgiveness.'

'Why? What have you done?' asked Busiris.

'You know what I've done,' she spat.

'Why don't you remind us both?'

'Eryx, please, don't listen to him! I'm just trying to say sorry.'

'Why, Evadne?' Eryx said quietly. 'What are you hoping to achieve?'

She clenched her fists by her sides, and closed her eyes.

'Nothing,' she said tightly and looked at him intently. 'I have no agenda. I just needed somebody to know that I'm not a damn monster.'

She whirled around and walked quickly out of the courtyard clearing, without looking back.

'Don't go after her, Eryx. She's trouble, for us all,' Busiris muttered.

Eryx said nothing, her words replaying in his head. *I just need someone to know I'm not a damn monster.* Someone? Or him?

'She nearly killed us, sabotaging the longboat. I would say I'm surprised she's chosen us as a refuge, but with you so willing to talk to her, I guess I can see why she'd try. She'll try Theseus next, you mark my words,' Busiris said.

It was like ice water being thrown over Eryx, dousing at once the spark of hope that had been kindling inside him. Busiris was right. Of course he was right. Evadne was a snake, deceitful and self-serving.

That really was the last time he would talk to her.

19

HEDONE

'Are you sure you don't want to eat?' Hedone asked.

Hercules shook his head.

'No. Let the fools feast,' he answered, glowering out at the dark desert beyond the cabana. Before she could reply, a flash of white light forced her to throw her hands in front of her face with a cry. A god? When she lowered them, hesitantly, she gasped and pushed herself from the bed onto her knees.

'Zeus,' she breathed, bowing her head.

'Father,' said Hercules. Hedone lifted her head and peeked at the lord of the gods. He was human sized, standing in the middle of the cabana and looking around in distaste. His hair and beard were shining silver, his body hard and lean in an ancient-style toga.

'Ares has some strange offspring,' he muttered. 'The Amazons are among the strangest. Women who don't want men are in no way normal.' Zeus looked at Hercules. 'I see you are doing a fine job of ignoring my instructions.'

'Asterion and Evadne have let me down,' Hercules said,

his teeth gritted. 'They are useless and too many of these Trials rely on more than one person.'

'Stop being such a child!' Zeus shouted at him. Hercules flinched but held the god's gaze and Hedone stared at him in awe. How did he have so much courage?

'I'm beginning to think that you do not want immortality, boy,' Zeus spat.

'Of course I do, I—'

Zeus cut him off.

'So, are you going to blame the others for your inability to beat Hippolyta today?'

Hercules pressed his lips together, his face reddening.

'I didn't think so,' Zeus said, folding his arms. 'I've enough to worry about, with Hades' insolence to deal with. I don't have time to spoon-feed you.'

'I'll do better, Father,' Hercules said stiffly.

'You'll do more than that, you'll win. The Trial is not about the tests, it's about who has the belt. Hippolyta will willingly give it to the victor tomorrow but if someone were to take it before then, they would be the winner.' Hedone didn't notice Zeus's patronising tone as his words sank in. 'If you weren't so busy feeling sorry for yourself, you'd have realised that already. I will not be able to help you again, Hercules. This is your last chance.' In another flash of white, the god was gone.

'He's right. Of course he's right,' Hedone said excitedly, scrabbling to her feet. Hercules looked at her, muscles still tense and face tight.

'One day I will be stronger than him,' he hissed. Alarm shot through Hedone at his words.

'Hercules, you mustn't say things like that,' she whispered. 'If he heard you...' She sat down beside him, and rubbed her hand up and down his arm. 'You must dress and go and find the belt. You can win this tonight!' She pushed playfully at his arm and his eyes softened.

'Yes. Yes, you're right. I can end this now,' he said slowly. 'Where is my lion skin?'

20

HERCULES

'What if the queen is wearing the belt?'

Hercules paused in strapping *Keravnos* to his hip, and looked at Hedone.

'I doubt it, at this time of night,' he said. 'It's late now, they'll all be asleep.' Idiots, every one of them, he thought. No doubt the feast had made them sleepy on stomachs full of wine and food.

'I just don't think it will be very easy to steal,' Hedone said, her voice full of soft concern.

'Hedone, my love, I will be back before you know it, as a winner. Then we can leave this accursed place and get back on the *Hybris*.'

She smiled at him.

'I would like that,' she said. He pulled her to him and she laughed her exquisite little giggle.

'Kiss me,' he breathed, and she did, deep and soft at the same time. He would never, ever tire of her kiss.

'Are you ready?' she said, as he reluctantly broke off their embrace and reached for his lion skin. He was more than ready, anticipation-fuelled power thrumming through his veins.

'Of course.'

'How will you know where she sleeps?'

'I'll find her,' he said, confidently. And if he couldn't, he'd make someone tell him where she was.

Hedone nodded at him.

'Can you keep the belt if you win?'

'I don't know.'

'I wonder if it would make me strong, like her.'

Hercules's face darkened.

'You don't want to be anything like her, Hedone. That's not what women were made to do.'

Hedone looked at him, thinking.

'Well, maybe I'd like just a little of her strength, then,' she said.

'You have my strength now. You do not need anything else.'

She beamed.

'See you shortly, my love,' he said, and ran down the steps of the cabana into the dark gardens.

HERCULES MADE his way through the gardens quickly, then crept along the palace wall, keeping to the shadows. Nobody was awake. He had not been entirely truthful about his plan to Hedone. He did intend to steal the belt, but not from Hippolyta's rooms as she slept. He had a score to settle with the vile woman. He would make her pay for what she had done to him, for making a fool of him. He touched his throat subconsciously as he looked up the high walls of the palace. Her rooms could be anywhere in the huge building, he'd be there all night looking for her. Unless... He smiled as the thought struck him.

He ran silently back through the gardens, pausing each time he reached one of the flickering lanterns hanging in the trees. One by one, he pulled open the glass containers and held the little candles under the leaves. When a few of them caught light, he dropped the candles under the branches and jogged quietly on to the next one.

21

LYSSA

'I still can't believe Hippolyta agreed to this,' Epizon said, pacing up and down Lyssa's cabana.

'Well, I can't believe you have the blood of Ares in you,' she answered, wringing her hands. His nervousness was infectious.

'Really? It's not hard to believe. Look at him!' Phyleus exclaimed.

Epizon laughed.

'I didn't know, I swear. I'll ask her about it tonight. If she ever gets here.' He looked out of the cabana again, towards the gardens, and drew in a sharp breath.

There she was, walking slowly towards them.

'Epizon,' Antiope said, as she reached the building. Lyssa and Phyleus backed away, Lyssa sitting down silently on a bed near the far end of the open-walled room.

'Mother,' Epizon said quietly. Antiope's eye twitched at the word.

'You look well,' she said, and climbed the steps.

'As do you.'

'Captain Lyssa tells me you are her first mate, and that you were recently wounded.'

Epizon nodded.

'And that Hercules was responsible?'

'Yes.'

'I do not like Hercules.'

'No. He is an evil man.'

They both fell silent. Their awkwardness was as infectious as their nerves had been and Lyssa watched uncomfortably as they avoided each other's gaze.

'How did you survive when I left?' Antiope asked suddenly.

'I fought in the pit. I was good.'

'How did you learn to fight?'

Epizon looked at her in surprise.

'Watching you. I watched you for years.'

'Oh. I didn't realise boys could learn so young.'

'Boys learn the same as girls,' he answered, and Antiope scoffed.

'No, they do not.'

'How would you know?' Epizon's words came out soft, but the sentiment was clear. Lyssa looked away, suddenly feeling like she was prying.

'I did not come here to be told that my way of life is wrong,' Antiope said, straightening up.

'I'm not saying it is wrong. I am saying there is much you don't know.'

Lyssa looked up again, waiting for Antiope to curse or leave, but she simply cocked her head at Epizon.

'This is true. But I have no desire for more knowledge. I am happy here.'

'I'm glad. I suppose that's all I wanted to hear,' Epizon said.

'That I am happy? Why does that matter to you?'

Epizon let out a long breath.

'It just does. I can't explain it to you, but I care.'

'Oh,' she said.

'As we're both here, though, there was one other thing... Do you know who my father is?'

Antiope stepped backwards, frowning.

'I will not talk of him. All you need to know is that he is dead.'

Lyssa resisted the urge to get up as she looked at Epizon's crestfallen face.

'Right,' he said, rubbing his brow, then looking at Antiope. 'Lyssa said you are descended from Ares?'

'Yes.'

'Why didn't you tell me? As a child?'

'I didn't think you would live long enough to care.'

This time pain did flash across Epizon's face.

'Then why did you bother keeping me alive?'

'I believed you might be useful at some point.'

Anger spiked inside Lyssa. Her respect for these people was dwindling fast. How could they be so cold?

'Epizon, understand that if you had been female, I would have loved you.'

'That doesn't help,' he said quietly.

Antiope frowned.

'Our people are very different,' she said eventually.

'I don't know who my people are,' Epizon said, his voice strained.

'We're your people,' Lyssa said, unable to help herself. She stood up. 'We're your people, Epizon. Nobody on the *Alastor* needs a parent's love to define them.' He gave her a grateful smile, and squared his shoulders a little.

'You're right, Captain.' He turned back to Antiope. 'I'm

glad to have met you,' he said formally. She just nodded at him.

'Thank you, Captain Lyssa,' she said, facing her.

'For what?'

Antiope didn't answer, but turned and walked slowly down the steps and away into the gardens.

LYSSA CLEARED the distance between her and Epizon quickly, and gave him the tenderest hug she could manage around his wounded chest.

'That was pretty brutal,' she said.

'I don't know what I was expecting,' he sighed. 'At the least, I thought I might find out who my father was.'

'Who needs that kind of information? It's not done Lyssa or me any good,' said Phyleus, bringing over a glass of wine. Epizon took it from him with a small smile.

'What did yours do?' he asked him.

'I'll tell you another time,' Phyleus answered, with a sideways glance at Lyssa.

'CAPTAIN!' The shout, accompanied by the sound of galloping hooves, made them all turn around. 'Captain, come quick,' panted Nestor, skidding to a halt by the cabana. 'The palace is on fire.'

Hercules dragged the beautiful Hippolyta from her fast horse by her hair, ready to use his fierce strength to wrestle the belt from the Amazon Queen, while the Maids of War watched.

EXCERPT FROM

THE FALL OF TROY BY QUINTUS SMYRNAEUS

Written 4 AD

Paraphrased by Eliza Raine

EVADNE

E vadne woke with a start, sitting up quickly on the cold stone bench. Everything was bathed in flickering orange light, and she could hear shouting in the distance. When had she fallen asleep? Tears had dried stiff on her cheeks and she rubbed at her face. A warrior ran past her.

'Wait!' Evadne called thickly. 'What's happening?'

'Fire!' the woman yelled back over her shoulder. Evadne stood up quickly, her head swimming slightly from the rapid movement, and followed after the Amazon.

IT WAS a good job she had woken up when she did. The fire had spread to the section of the garden next to her crew's cabana, the tall green plants roaring with flames. When she looked to her right, towards the palace, she was shocked to see the flames licking at the stone walls, climbing high.

'Hippolyta!' roared a familiar voice. Her blood curdled inside her. Hercules. Was he responsible for this? 'Face me, you coward!' he bellowed again.

Every sane part of Evadne wanted to turn and run, away from his voice, away from the flames. But her feet moved of their own accord, further towards the palace.

HERCULES WAS STANDING in the middle of a courtyard, the trees and plants once surrounding it now burned to a crisp, the flames moving on to fresh fuel. He was wielding *Keravnos* and was dressed for battle. Amazons in metal helmets and gauntlets had formed a circle around him and were side-stepping so that it gradually tightened like a noose. A crowd was forming beyond the ring.

'You send your warriors to do your job because you fear me!' Hercules laughed as he shouted, holding his sword high. There was a thud, and the circle of women parted. Hippolyta stepped through, her eyes blazing as they bored into Hercules.

'This time, it is to the death,' she hissed.

'I agree,' he said, smiling. His other hand shot out from under his cloak and there was a small metallic sound, then Hippolyta staggered backwards, her hands flying to a bolt embedded in her stomach. Evadne stared at the weapon in Hercules's hand, recognising it as a crossbow. The Amazons around them froze as blood spread fast across Hippolyta's bare midriff. Hercules was on her in an instant, gripping her short hair and drawing back her head.

'You have some advanced weapons in these gardens, my queen,' he hissed, raising his sword to her neck. She gasped, still clutching her stomach. The tall Amazon that had fought Antaeus earlier cried out and began to run towards him. 'One more step and I will kill her!' he shouted.

The woman slowed, fury on her face.

'If you kill her, you won't get the belt,' a male voice said.

'Theseus, no!' Hippolyta choked, as Theseus stepped into the courtyard, holding up a wide leather strap, shining with metal chain links.

'Let her go, and I'll give you the belt.'

Hercules stared at him.

'How did you get it?' he snarled.

'She gave it to me. We are... old friends.' The warriors around them gasped, frowning and muttering.

'Theseus, stop,' breathed Hippolyta.

'It's too late, my love. I will not see you die.'

Theseus and Hippolyta? Evadne stared.

'My love? Is it true, my queen? You are in love with a man?' the tall Amazon asked, her voice disbelieving.

Hippolyta closed her eyes as Hercules yanked her head back further.

'Enough!' he barked. 'If you have the belt, Theseus, then you have already won. Even more reason to kill this freak.'

'I concede,' said Theseus, quickly. 'I withdraw. Just let her go.'

'You withdraw from the whole competition?'

'Yes.'

Hercules narrowed his eyes for a moment, and Hippolyta took a ragged breath.

'Let her go, now,' Theseus said.

'Toss me the belt.'

'Let her go first. You know I am a man of my word.'

Hercules only hesitated a moment more, before shoving the woman towards Theseus. Theseus dropped to his knees to catch her, throwing the belt at Hercules as he did so.

'Help me,' he said, struggling to hold Hippolyta as blood gushed from her wound, but the women around them just stared.

A sudden roar erupted from the tall woman, and she

threw herself at Hercules as he stooped to pick up the belt. He stood up quickly, thrusting his sword out as she collided with him, and Evadne heard a man shout as *Keravnos* slid effortlessly through the woman's chest. The blood-covered tip of the sword protruded through her back and Evadne spun away, sure she was going to empty the contents of her stomach onto the ground.

'Amazons, attack! Kill the outsiders!'

The call was followed by a cacophony of battle cries, and Evadne's eyes widened in fear as she realised the Amazons weren't just charging at Hercules. They were charging at them all.

THANK YOU

Thank you so much for reading, I hope you enjoyed it! If so, you would absolutely make my day if you could leave me a review on Amazon, they help me out so much! You can do that here.

If you want to find out what happened when Lyssa and her crew went to Leo to pick up Tenebrae then you can read the exclusive short story, Winds of Olympus, by signing up for my newsletter here. You'll also be the first to know about new releases!

Fires of Olympus concludes the series and is available here!

Made in the USA
Monee, IL
05 May 2021

67759751R00152